Rhyme and the Runaway Twins

Chicken GIRLS

MYSTERY 1

Rhyme and the Runaway Twins

MATILDA HIGGINS

Sky Pony Press
New York

Sky Pony Press books may be purchased in bulk at special discounts for sales promotion, corporate gifts, fund-raising, or educational purposes. Special editions can also be created to specifications. For details, contact the Special Sales Department, Sky Pony Press, 307 West 36th Street, 11th Floor, New York, NY 10018 or info@skyhorsepublishing.com.

Sky Pony® is a registered trademark of Skyhorse Publishing, Inc.®, a Delaware corporation. Visit our website at www.skyponypress.com.

10 9 8 7 6 5 4 3 2 1

Library of Congress Cataloging-in-Publication Data is available on file.

Print ISBN: 978-1-5107-4218-5
Ebook ISBN: 978-1-5107-4219-2

Cover design by Brian Peterson
Cover illustration by Bethany Straker

Printed in the United States of America

Rhyme and the Runaway Twins

Summer, 2018

PROLOGUE

"Attaway's not the sort of place you hang around for very long . . ." The line played over and over in Meg's head as their station wagon clattered over a streak of potholes and past a green sign that read: ATTAWAY—POP. 39,674. She glanced to the passenger seat and nudged Conrad's shoulder. "We're here," she said to her sleeping brother.

"I was hoping you'd just wake me up when we're headed home," said Conrad, as he fumbled for his glasses. "And done with this wild-goose chase."

What home? Meg thought to herself. "C'mon, Conrad. This is our only chance," she scolded him. When her brother said nothing, Meg stepped on the gas, giving the car a nasty jolt.

As the town came into sight, Meg thought again about the letter. *Not the sort of place you hang around for very long.* Maybe so, but at this point, Attaway was their only hope. If nothing turned up here, Meg wasn't sure what they would do. The summer was dwindling fast.

"Anything from Uncle Fiske?" Conrad finally mumbled.

"He won't notice we're gone until he's finished appraising every square inch of that house," Meg said, stopping at a traffic light across from the town green. *This* was the place no one wanted to hang around? From Meg's point of view, it looked pleasant enough. A few kids leaving an arcade, an old clock tower bent at the hip, and coming around the corner, a pretty girl all in pink.

"Welcome to Attaway," Meg said to her brother.

CHAPTER 1

The town library was a quaint brick building next to the church and across from the fire station. It had an American flag out front and, in spring and summer, rows of white, pink, and blue geraniums that perfumed the stone path to the front doors. Inside, the children's section shone with primary colors and cardboard displays of literary greats like Stuart Little, Paddington Bear, and Dr. Seuss. Just behind that was the teen lounge—a few high tables and a giant blue bean bag near the window. Beyond that was the periodical room, where Rhyme McAdams was sneezing her way through a big box of dusty archives.

"Bless you, dear," Ms. Sharpe said, as she opened an embossed letter from that day's mail. "And bless *us*! I can't believe my eyes, but it looks like a donor has given a very generous contribution to the Attaway County Fair!"

Ms. Sharpe was Rhyme's friend Kayla's mom, as well as the town librarian and "official Attaway historian"—though Rhyme couldn't for the life of her think of anything worth remembering about her hometown. And yet here she was, on summer break, stuck sifting through the town's archives. A few months earlier, Rhyme had failed her school's practice exam (better known as the "Test Test"). In exchange for helping out around the library, Ms. Sharpe had agreed to tutor Rhyme in all of the subjects she'd flunked last spring.

"Oh yeah?" Rhyme said, hoping the donor might distract Ms. Sharpe from their impending trigonometry session. "Who sent the donation?" Rhyme asked, rising up on her tiptoes to peek over Ms. Sharpe's shoulder. *From the desk of Silas Manderley*, was written in curly letterhead at the top.

"Nobody you'd know," Ms. Sharpe answered curtly, looking up. "Are you already done with that box? Because we have a date with our good friends *sine, cosine,* and *tangent* coming up momentarily."

Rhyme sighed and shook her head; it was going to be another long day. Ms. Sharpe was curating an "Attaway Retrospective" exhibit at the county fair this summer, and Rhyme had been tasked with reading through ancient newspapers to find stories that might be "of general interest." Which was funny, Rhyme thought, considering there was absolutely nothing interesting about Attaway—then or now.

Five days a week, Rhyme sat at the same round table, facing the back courtyard, bent over a huge stack of yellowing papers. Today she wore a rose-colored summer dress and white slip-on sneakers. Her brown hair hung in two long braids. Doe-eyed and sincere,

Rhyme was often described by adults as "the girl next door." Maybe it was intended as a compliment, but what Rhyme heard was *young, quiet, unassuming*. She had never craved the spotlight, but that didn't mean she wanted to be overlooked.

And speaking of overlooked, Rhyme forced herself to focus on the task at hand. In the past few weeks, she had learned more about Attaway than she'd ever cared to know. Fallout shelters. Scandalous "miniskirts", which didn't seem all that mini. Someone from Attaway who came in tenth at an international yo-yo contest. A new fondue restaurant that opened in 1974. The basketball game versus Millwood where the marching band was suspended for performing a Beatles' song instead of the national anthem.

"Look at those beehives," said a voice behind Rhyme. It was Matilda, an older girl from school. Until last year, Matilda had been the editor-in-chief of the school paper. She was in her usual black overalls, with a gray Attaway High T-shirt underneath. She wore her hair loose and un-styled, constantly tucking it behind her ears as she whizzed through the Dewey decimal system. Miraculously, Matilda actually seemed to enjoy their surroundings.

"Sorry?" Rhyme asked.

"*That* hairstyle," Matilda said, pointing out a blond pouf from a photograph of the 1967 "Groovy" Fall Ball.

"Oh, right," Rhyme said, tugging at her own braids self-consciously. She'd never heard of a "beehive" before.

"And that's my section," Matilda said, reaching over and gathering up all of the clippings spread out on the desk.

"I guess you're welcome then," Rhyme said with a weak grin. "More work for me and less for you."

"Actually, you're wrong," said Matilda, bringing the papers over to the other side of the table. "Now it's even more work for me." She scrambled around in her bag for a pen. "You totally messed up the order."

"That might be a *little* bit of an exaggeration," Rhyme said, holding her thumb and pointer finger just a tiny bit apart. But Matilda was no longer looking at her.

"Do you spend a lot of time with archival materials while you're practicing your handstands?" Matilda said under her breath, jotting something down in her notebook.

"I'm a dancer," said Rhyme, trying to make her voice as pleasant as possible. "Not a gymnast."

"Whatever floats your boat." Matilda rearranged a bunch of red leather yearbooks. Rhyme sighed. This was officially going to be the most boring summer of her life.

CHAPTER 2

Later that evening, Rhyme walked home, exhausted from the day of sinusoidal functions and sixties hairdos. She glanced at her phone—no new messages. No gossip, no selfies, nobody to commiserate with about her miserable summer. It felt as if all of Rhyme's friends had abandoned Attaway for the break. Ellie and Kayla were back at the dance camp where they'd first met last year. Quinn was staying with her dad for the summer. Rooney and Birdie were traveling through Alaska on a teen tour. Even the PowerSurge girls had disappeared for family trips and study abroad programs.

And then there was T. K., who had waited until the night of the Spring Fling, the night they shared their very first kiss, to announce that he'd been accepted to an internship all the way out in Los Angeles. T. K. and his friend Flash were staying with Flash's dad—a big-shot director in Hollywood—and learning to make movies.

Earlier in the summer, Rhyme and T. K. had exchanged a few texts and calls, mostly about how sunny it was in California and how boring it was in Attaway. But now, it had been over a week since they'd talked. Then again, why would T. K. want to hear about Ms. Sharpe and the county fair, when he was probably surrounded by glamorous celebrities at fancy parties? Rhyme was happy for T. K.— he was off having the summer of his life. But she couldn't help but feel like, once again, they were stuck in some kind of in-between.

As she turned down her street, Rhyme sighed and looked around her neighborhood. Row after row of nearly identical houses stood empty, hardly any cars in the driveways, few lights turned on. The power lines crackled in the heat, and she could hear the faint sound of a jet engine, the plane cabin probably filled with people going somewhere way more exciting. Outside of old Mrs. Simpson's place, an unfamiliar station wagon was parked too far from the curb. Mrs. Simpson had been Rhyme's neighbor her entire life. Growing up, the old woman had always babysat Rhyme and Harmony—until last year, when Rhyme finally convinced her parents she was old enough to stay home alone. Rhyme passed the car, hoping it meant Ellie or Quinn had hitched a ride home early. But the plates read NORTH CAROLINA. *Weird*, Rhyme thought, as she headed up her driveway. Who would ever take a trip *to* Attaway?

Rhyme opened the front door and kicked off her shoes. She plunked down on the comfy ottoman, staring out the window. The fireflies hadn't come out yet. *At least I still have my family. They'll hang out with me*, Rhyme thought. In the summers Rhyme and her family would walk to the town green, laying out a picnic and catching the shimmering insects in Mason jars. Harmony never wanted to let them go, but Rhyme always liberated the insects, for fear that their lights might go out forever. Rhyme smiled. Maybe there were still things to look forward to that summer. Her mom's chicken salad. Iced tea. She'd even be willing to sit on the back porch with her dad and his telescope, as he droned on about Scorpius and Lyra and all of the other summer constellations.

Just then, Rhyme's father came barreling down the staircase, looking totally frazzled. Rhyme noticed a pile of suitcases sitting by the landing. "What's all this?" she asked her dad.

"Didn't Mom tell you?" Her dad looked exasperated. "Here, can you sit on this to get it to shut?" he said, gesturing at a bulging bag.

"Are we going somewhere?" Rhyme asked hopefully.

Her father, a slight, serious man with brown eyes like Rhyme's, looked guiltily at the floor. "I'm sorry, honey, but Harmony's rehearsal schedule moved up two weeks." Rhyme stood still for a second, and then turned away from her father, already knowing what was coming. "Your mom and I need to take her to LA tonight, and we won't be back until Labor Day."

Before she could respond, Rhyme's sister sashayed down the stairs. Dressed to the nines in a turquoise halter top, sparkly black pants, and white sunglasses, Harmony's curly hair was straightened past her shoulders. "No photos, please," she cooed at her older sister. "I'm simply *not* camera ready." Rhyme rolled her eyes. Their mom, following in Harmony's footsteps, rushed to hold the door, as if the precocious nine-year-old was a *really big deal*.

The problem was, Harmony *was* sort of a big deal. That spring, she had been discovered by a casting agent in Malibu for a new TV show called *Hotel du Loone*. Playing a kid detective named Jazzy, Harmony had filmed a pilot episode earlier in the summer, to see if the network executives liked the idea. Apparently they were so impressed with her acting that they were bringing Harmony back to film an entire season. Rhyme could only imagine how much her tiny sister's ego would balloon once the show actually started airing on TV.

It took over an hour to pack up the car. By then, Rhyme's dad was in a sweat, and her mom was huffing and puffing about missing their flight. Harmony, meanwhile, lounged in the back seat, firing off texts to her castmates. Suddenly she was using phrases like *babe* and *sweetie*. When she wasn't applying lip gloss, with exaggerated, pouty smacks, Harmony fired off orders to their parents. "I wanted the rainbow scrunchie!" she screeched through the open car window, hardly looking up from her phone. Before they drove off into the sunset, Rhyme's parents came over to the stoop, where Rhyme had been sitting in a daze.

"Look on the bright side," said Rhyme's mom, as she pulled her dark brown hair into a bun. "Mrs. Simpson has a diving board, and if you want to have any of your friends stay over, you officially have her permission." She smiled at Rhyme's dad, who nodded with encouragement. "You're staying at Mrs. Simpson's," her mother said, as if she had already told Rhyme this. Which she definitely had *not*. "It's perfect, actually. She broke her hip this spring and is still having some trouble getting around."

"WHAT?! I thought we decided I could stay home by myself last year!"

"Not overnight, dear," her father said, shaking his head as if it were ridiculous. "Mrs. Simpson's doing us a huge favor."

"Why can't I just come with you?" Rhyme said, not bothering to listen to her parents lecture her once again on school and the library and "responsibility."

"You know we would bring you if we could," her dad said. "But if you don't pass your exams in the fall, the school said you might have to repeat a grade."

"So that means studying with Ms. Sharpe," her mom chimed in. "Here's some pocket money in case you need it, though I happen to know Mrs. Simpson is an excellent cook." She handed Rhyme an envelope stuffed with dollar bills.

"Don't spend it all in one place!" her dad laughed. Rhyme rolled her eyes.

"Remember to thank Mrs. Simpson," her mom added. "And to help with Reggie!" Rhyme had almost forgotten about Mrs. Simpson's yapping Boston terrier.

"Great. Another chore. Just what I needed," Rhyme tried to say, pocketing the envelope, which felt more like a bribe than spending money. But her parents had wrapped her in a bear hug, muffling her complaints.

"We'll call you every day before bed!" her mom said, as they hurried off to the car. "Love you!"

Rhyme stood to watch as the car pulled out. Through the open window, Harmony blew her a series of kisses.

So much for fireflies, Rhyme thought. Across the way, she saw that the station wagon in front of Mrs. Simpson's had vanished. It hadn't taken long for the unknown visitors to realize they were better off in North Carolina. With a sigh, Rhyme sat down by the rose bushes that separated her house from Mrs. Simpson's.

Inhaling deeply, Rhyme paused and pulled out her phone. Quickly, she typed up a text to T. K. "Hey. Harmony and my parents are on the way to LA Maybe u will see them." For a long moment, she waited to see the three dots that told her he was writing back. But there were no dots.

It had always been like this with T. K. Maybe yes, maybe no.

CHAPTER 3

The next day at the library, Rhyme was tasked with organizing Attaway High report cards from 1960–1963. Everybody had such formal names back then, Rhyme noticed, like *Melvin* and *Lawrence* and *Gertrude*. She wondered what they'd think of *Kayla* and *Flash*. At least one thing hadn't changed: bad grades. One girl, Alice Hargrove, had a C-minus average in the spring of 1962—good luck to *her* on the Test Test!

"Makes you look like a Rhodes Scholar," said a voice over Rhyme's shoulder. Matilda. Sometimes it was like she could read Rhyme's mind. "Why are *you* reading report cards?" Matilda said.

Was she making small talk?

"Maybe Ms. Sharpe is a hoarder," Rhyme ventured, with a small grin.

"I wasn't trying to bad-mouth Ms. Sharpe," Matilda said curtly. "She had asked *me* to catalog those yesterday, and it looks like you're interfering again."

Rhyme's ears grew hot. "She asked me to put these in order. Not you," said Rhyme, all of a sudden filled with anger. "So why don't you mind your own business?"

"Because this *is* my business," Matilda snarled. "Unlike you, this is a summer job for me. I'm not some spoiled little girl whose parents pay for everything." Matilda's icy glare moved to Rhyme's purse, where three twenty-dollar bills stuck out like ducks' tails.

"If you're so obsessed with organization, have it your way!" Rhyme pushed the pile at Matilda, upsetting the neat stacks.

Rhyme stormed off to the library's entryway, to tell Ms. Sharpe that she refused to work next to Matilda. What was her problem? It wasn't Rhyme's fault that Matilda needed to earn money! As she rounded the hallway, Rhyme balled up her fists and bit her lower lip—she simply could not work under these conditions! But as she turned the corner, she saw that Ms. Sharpe was not alone.

"I'm sorry," the librarian was saying, "but you absolutely cannot access historical records without a library card."

"What's wrong with a driver's license?" said an older-looking girl, with olive skin and the greenest eyes Rhyme had ever seen. The girl leaned toward Ms. Sharpe with one hand on the desk, making her seem commanding—threatening, even. Rhyme was intimidated, and hung back, hidden by a graphic novel display.

"Unfortunately," said Ms. Sharpe, "you can't get a library card without an Attaway address. And yours is from Virginia." She handed back the license.

"Well, isn't that perfect," the girl huffed, turning to her companion. Rhyme guessed he was probably her boyfriend. She couldn't see his face, but he was tall, with skinny blue jeans and a backwards cap sporting a logo for some sort of Wildlife Fund. He looked to be about the girl's age, but his deeply tanned arms were covered in tattoos. Rhyme had never known anyone her age with a tattoo, let alone someone with two arms full of them. These two were definitely not from around here.

"Hold on a second, Meg," said the boy. "Is there anything we can do?" His voice was sweeter, more cajoling than the girl's. "We've only just gotten into town, and it would mean a lot to us."

"What brings you to Attaway?" Ms. Sharpe asked sternly.

"Visiting our cousin," said the girl—Meg—a little too quickly, like she was covering up something. "We're just here for a week or two," she added. *Our* cousin, Rhyme noted. So they were related.

"Then perhaps you could use your cousin's card?" Ms. Sharpe said, neatening up a row of bookmarks on the counter. "And just who is your cousin?" But Meg was already pulling her bag onto her shoulder and turning away.

"Thanks for all your help," she said, with an edge of sarcasm.

The boy hung back. "Seriously, we appreciate the time." When he turned to leave, Rhyme caught a glimpse of his face.

High cheekbones, full lips. He was remarkably attractive, Rhyme thought, blushing. But more significantly, the boy looked exactly like Meg. They weren't just brother and sister, Rhyme realized. They were twins.

As they left, Rhyme slipped out from behind the display, intrigued by the mysterious new transplants. *Wouldn't it be nice,* she thought, *to have a confidante my own age?* Rhyme drew closer to the broad, dusty window to get a better look. Meg, she saw, was pulling out a large map (hadn't they heard of the Internet?) and jabbing at it with her pointer finger. Rhyme cracked the window slightly, curious where the cryptic pair were headed.

"That's it, Conrad. I'm telling you," Meg said, "we don't need property records."

The boy shook his head. "But that doesn't match the letter."

"Just trust me," she said, groaning in frustration. "Come on, let's go."

The twins continued to the parking lot, to the same car that had been idling outside Mrs. Simpson's. *Of course it was theirs.* The red station wagon from North Carolina. Conrad looked up to see Rhyme at the window. They locked eyes. Or at least she thought they did. Then he jumped in, and the mysterious twins zoomed off.

Before she could process this all, Ms. Sharpe called out: "Rhyme! It's that time again! Trigonometry time!" As her tutor approached, Rhyme's phone buzzed in her pocket. A new message. But just as she was going to reach for it, Ms. Sharpe stopped her.

"You'll have plenty of time to play with your phone later," said Ms. Sharpe, pressing a workbook and protractor into Rhyme's reluctant hands. "For the next hour, all you have to worry about are Pythagorean identities."

CHAPTER 4

Rhyme dug a spoon into a carton of mint chip ice cream. Dinner. Mrs. Simpson spent Fridays at the Sunset Club, a senior citizen club nearby that ran weekly bingo games, and she wouldn't be back until later. All alone, Rhyme had decided to make the most of a house with no adults. *Two* houses with no adults, she reminded herself, as she turned up the volume on Mrs. Simpson's surprisingly high-tech stereo system.

After coming home from the library, Rhyme had walked Reggie, the old Boston terrier that really preferred to be carried. Aside from the drivers of passing cars, the only other person Rhyme saw was the gardener, a not-so-friendly man about her dad's age, who tended the rosebushes once a week.

Finally, he drove off in his pickup truck, and Rhyme made herself right at home. In particular with Mrs. Simpson's fancy speakers.

Her parents would've killed her for blasting music this loud. You could probably hear it down the street. *Another perk of being the only person left on the block*, Rhyme thought, as she dug into the dessert course: a bag of extra-spicy jalapeño chips. Over the booming music, she couldn't even hear herself chew. Or think. And that was a plus.

All afternoon, during the long, grueling study session, Rhyme's thoughts had drifted anywhere and everywhere . . . except of course to the math problems at hand. Over at the library, Ms. Sharpe had charged her with completing a problem set on the "practical applications" of trigonometry. Namely, calculating the time it would take for a car driving sixty miles per hour at a thirty-degree angle to collide with a train traveling forty miles per hour. Rhyme couldn't find anything practical about the problem. Who would ever drive a car *toward* a moving train?

While she penciled and erased numbers, Rhyme couldn't help but imagine a red station wagon careening through Attaway. In the driver's seat, the beautiful girl with green eyes perched cat-eye sunglasses on her forehead. And her handsome brother sat beside her, his tattooed arm hanging out the passenger side window, dark brown against the red paint. Both of them kept their eyes locked on the horizon. By and by, the town melted away, leaving an open highway that began to cut through a never-ending desert. In the distance, an old locomotive sounded its whistle in warning. As the train snaked along the tracks, closer and closer, the boy attempted to jerk the steering wheel and avert a collision. But the girl couldn't be stopped, slamming her foot down on the pedal. Into the wind, she screamed, "Property records!"

"Earth to Rhyme!" Ms. Sharpe had admonished her, rousing Rhyme from her daydreams. "It's opposite *over* the hypotenuse. Not adjacent." Kayla's mom had seemed at her wit's end, like Rhyme was a lost cause. Which, as she hit rock bottom of the ice cream carton, Rhyme now worried wasn't far from the truth. . . .

Just then, her cell phone rang. Mom. Rhyme rushed to turn down the volume on the stereo.

"Rhyme?" Her mother's voice sounded muffled and far away. "Hold on, honey, I'm putting you on speakerphone. I'm with Dad and Harmony." From the background, they chorused, "How was your day?"

"Oh, fine," Rhyme said glumly. "I got in a fight with Matilda and screwed up my trig assignment."

"You'll get there, kiddo!" said her dad. "How's the house? How's Mrs. Simpson? Both still standing?" He chuckled on the other end of the line.

"Everything's fine here. Same old . . ." Rhyme said, failing to mention that Mrs. Simpson's active social life meant Rhyme was basically staying home alone anyway. "Actually, there *are* these two new kids who showed up today without a library card . . ."

"New friends?" Her dad sounded distracted. "That's wonderful, honey! Hold on. Here's Harmony. She wants to say hi, too."

"Rhyme, darling!" Her sister came on the line, a faux British accent in tow. "Tell me about your new companions!"

"What? I'm not friends with them," Rhyme said, trying not to sound too annoyed. "Are you guys even listening?"

"To your every word, babes," said Harmony. "Tell me everything."

"Well, I've never seen anybody like them in Attaway. I think they're brother and sister. Twins, maybe. The boy even has tattoos all over his arms. They could be celebrities—do you know any famous twins? Or maybe they're on the run, like criminals or outlaws," Rhyme said breathlessly.

"Just like Bonnie and Clyde," Harmony chuckled, in a knowing way that made Rhyme feel small.

"Who?"

"You *really* need to watch the classics, sis." Harmony sighed. "So, the funniest thing happened between takes today . . ." As Harmony began to recount her daily schedule on set, the reception went fuzzy.

"Hello?"

" . . .*and the lady who plays Mrs. Moorehouse told me . . .*"

"Harmony?"

" . . .*which made Toby get the hiccups, and . . .*"

"I can't hear you!"

"Sorry, kiddo." Her dad's voice came on the line. "Bad service here. Can we try you back from the hotel?"

"Don't worry about it," Rhyme said. "I'm going to sleep soon anyway."

Hanging up, Rhyme noticed a little red balloon hovering above her messages. The text from earlier. She'd grown so accustomed to radio silence that she rarely checked her inbox anymore.

But there it was: one new notification.

She swiped with her thumb, and a message from T. K. popped up. Her heart rose in her chest, and then plummeted all the way to Mrs. Simpson's basement. She tried responding, but her thumbs were paralyzed. And just like that, Rhyme was transported back to that magical night from a few months ago, when the stars had all aligned. . . .

She had come home from the Spring Fling, having snuck into the dance despite failing the Test Test. In the backyard, T. K. had set up bright lamps and a film projector, playing old videos of them together. It was perfect. And as they held hands in the moonlight, Rhyme believed it would go on like that forever. No more confusion, no more second-guessing. But then T. K. revealed his summer plans. He was abandoning her. Nearly in tears, she fled to the house. But he called out after her. Filled with conflicting emotions—like the hot and cold currents of the ocean—she rushed to his side. They kissed then, and nothing else seemed to matter.

Now that same, sweet boy had only this to say: "Ha no way."

Three measly, pathetic words. Days of complete silence, and that was all he texted in response to her message about her family going to LA. With a sigh, Rhyme tossed her phone away and curled up on Mrs. Simpson's couch. Beneath her, Reggie tucked in under the coffee table, his long black ears folding lazily. In a few minutes, Rhyme was sound asleep, back on that endless highway with the train tooting its whistle many miles away. . . .

A few hours later, Rhyme woke up with a start. It was nearly midnight, and Mrs. Simpson was fast asleep. (Rhyme could hear her legendary snores drifting softly from upstairs.) A soft sliding sound cut the silence, and Reggie stood up, on alert. "Shhh! Shhh, boy!" she whispered. Silence again. Maybe she had hallucinated the entire thing. But then, again, she heard the sliding sound. With a sickening jolt, Rhyme realized what it was.

A window opening, and a window closing.

CHAPTER 5

Creak!

Upstairs, the floorboards groaned as Rhyme sat paralyzed with fear. Mrs. Simpson slept like a log . . . and what were the chances Reggie knew how to open and close a window? It had to be somebody else—somebody who didn't belong. Rhyme was right in the intruder's sight line when they hit the stairs. There was no way to escape.

Rhyme backed into the pantry, her every muscle alert. She could have heard a pin drop down the block. As she shuffled back, seeking a good place to hide, she bumped against the shelves. A box of cereal fell to the ground. Loudly.

The footsteps stopped overhead.

Rhyme held her breath, sure the psycho killer could hear her heart beating. Who would break into Mrs. Simpson's? Suddenly she remembered the gardener, with his inky black eyes and permanent frown. Rhyme had to get out. With slow, cautious steps, she tried to tiptoe out of the pantry. *Crunch!* She'd stepped on the cereal. A loud footstep heaved onto the floorboards.

Scurrying into the hallway, Rhyme pulled open the first door she saw, stepped in, and closed the door gingerly so the latch didn't make a noise. Feeling around for something, anything, she let herself exhale. The strong stench of mothballs. She was practically drowning in Mrs. Simpson's fur coats. Running her hands over the minks and sables, she felt something long, thin, and heavy. A cane. Instinctively, she grabbed it, readying it in her hand like an all-star slugger.

There was nothing to do now but listen. Rhyme held her breath.

The steps were drawing nearer, and again she thought of the old train in the desert. Closer and closer. Her palms were sweating. She tightened her grip on the cane. Then, through a crack of blue light beneath the closet door—a reflection from the pool—she saw a pair of feet. He was right outside.

Rhyme closed her eyes. This was it. Fight or flight. And flight was no longer an option. *Or get kidnapped*, Rhyme thought, as the door swung open. In a single motion, Rhyme jumped out, pulled back the cane, which she now saw was a flimsy plastic—and delivered a strong blow against the intruder's shin.

"Ow!" he cried, as he crumpled to the ground.

Rhyme held up the cane for another line drive, when another voice interrupted. "Stop! Please! Don't!" A pair of hands flew up in the air. Another figure came into the light, and Rhyme realized . . .

"You!" she and Meg yelled at the same time.

"And me," said the intruder, now revealed to be Meg's brother. He was nursing his leg. "Conrad. And you're that girl from the library."

Rhyme wasn't ready to relinquish the cane, but she lowered it a little.

"You shouldn't use your real name, you dummy," Meg practically spat at her brother.

"I already know your name," Rhyme said. "Meg." Rhyme looked straight at her. Meg's face registered shock, then confirmation. Her eyes narrowed. Rhyme knew she had Meg backed into a corner, and what do cornered animals do but—

"Run!" Meg yelled, as she tried to shove Rhyme to the side. But Rhyme was quicker than she looked, twirling past her, and slamming the cane across the front door. Meg nearly clotheslined herself.

"You're not going anywhere until you tell me what's happening," Rhyme said.

"What?" Meg said, cocking her head. "You think you can stop both of us? What are you? Eleven? Twelve?"

Thirteen, Rhyme thought, indignant.

"We're not going anywhere until I make sure my shinbone isn't shattered," Conrad said, hobbling to his feet to take a seat at the kitchen table. "Thanks for that, by the way." Rhyme looked at Conrad, clearly not a seasoned criminal. And she almost felt bad for hurting him. But not that bad. With her free hand, she pulled out her phone, dialed, and turned it so it faced the twins, making sure the digits were visible: 911. Her thumb hovered over the Call button.

"Five seconds to tell me who you are and what's going on," she said. Conrad looked to Meg, who shook her head imperceptibly. "Five, four, three, two . . ." Rhyme turned the phone back again, so it was facing only her. " . . . one." Rhyme said as she tapped randomly at the bottom of her screen, making it look like she'd pressed Call.

"Okay, okay!" Meg waved her hands in the air. "Just hang up."

Rhyme, now very much in control—*and liking it*—pocketed her phone and pointed the cane at Mrs. Simpson's couch. "Good thing I have nothing but time."

The siblings shuffled over to the living room.

"First off," Rhyme said, "where are you from?"

"North Carolina," said Meg. Perched on the large, winged sofa, Meg reminded her of Birdie.

"Asheville," Conrad added from the recliner, set all the way back, the footrest elevating his injured leg. "You can't just tell people North Carolina. That's misleading."

"Does she even . . ." Meg turned to Rhyme. "Do you even know Asheville?" Rhyme shook her head no.

"It's a super cool town," Conrad explained. "Lots of converted warehouses and restaurants and live music."

"If it's so great, then why are you in boring Attaway?"

Conrad started to speak, but Meg flashed a look of warning in his direction.

"Weren't you eavesdropping in the library?" Meg's lips curled sarcastically. "You should know we're visiting our cousin for the summer."

"Is your cousin Mrs. Simpson?" The name didn't seem to register with either sibling. "Because you're trespassing in her house right now." Rhyme crossed her arms confidently.

Conrad said, "This house didn't always belong to her. It used to belong to our grandmother Bea. Or at least we think . . ."

"Cut it out, Conrad!" Meg hissed.

"Maybe she can help us . . ." Conrad said.

"*She* is me. Rhyme. And maybe I can help with what?"

"Finding out if this is really Grandma Bea's place," Conrad said. "We've never even set foot in Attaway before."

They all jumped in their seats as a door slammed shut upstairs. "Don't move, and don't make a sound," Rhyme said, running to the foot of the stairs. Reggie started barking furiously.

Mrs. Simpson called downstairs: "Rhyme, dear, everything all right? I heard a commotion down there." Slowly but surely, Mrs. Simpson descended the staircase, her curlers coming undone with every step. Before Rhyme could answer, Mrs. Simpson pushed past her and hobbled into the living room. "Wait! I can explain!" Rhyme said, running after the old lady, who was surprisingly spry, even with her cane. But the living room was empty. Out of the corner of her eye, Rhyme saw the back door was slightly ajar.

Meg and Conrad were gone.

CHAPTER 6

A few days later, a postcard from Camp Songbird arrived at Rhyme's house.

Rhyme!

We miss you! Everything at camp has been ah-mazing so far—except that you aren't here! Boo! Plus, there's no reception in the mountains so we can't even text. Double boo! You would love the rehearsal space here. It makes our gym look like a fast food place bathroom. They even have a recording studio! Oh! Also! You'll never believe it, but we're kinda bonding with PowerSurge. And I'm thinking about getting back into dance! We might even

*choreograph a routine for the end-of-summer
jamboree! I know. Crazy. Miss you so so so so so
so so so so so so much,*

XO, Ellie

Rhyme sighed, feeling a mix of happy, sad, and jealous as she read and reread the note. On the front of the postcard, a picture of a log cabin next to a shimmering lake looked exactly like summer was supposed to. Ellie had also included, in the envelope, a picture of her bunkmates wearing war paint and forest green handkerchiefs, their arms around each other's shoulders.

They looked to be having so much fun—and all getting along. Before school let out, the Chicken Girls and PowerSurge had put aside their longtime rivalry to dance together at the Spring Fling. The postcard made them look like old friends. And how about Ellie getting back into dance? She had dropped out last year, and Rhyme missed her best friend on the dance floor. With a big grin, she remembered their first collaboration, to "Rockin' Around the Christmas Tree" at the neighborhood holiday party. They couldn't have been more than seven or eight. But it seemed like a million years ago.

Rhyme's reveries were interrupted by a phone call. Seeing who it was, she picked up immediately.

"Birdie?"

"Rhyme? Hi!" What sounded like explosions erupted in the background. "Sorry I missed your call last week," Birdie said. "It's been a crazy summer."

"Where are you?" said Rhyme. "I can barely hear you."

"My bad. I'm still with my parents in Texas," she said. "There's all kinds of family drama happening down here, and of course baby bro left me all alone to deal with it."

"T. K. How, uh, is he?" She hoped Birdie couldn't hear the desperation in her voice.

Birdie laughed. "Way better than I am. Cruising around LA and going to fancy parties with Flash's dad. But I'm sure you know that already. Haven't you guys been talking?"

Not knowing what to say, Rhyme tried to change the topic. "Is everything all right in Texas? I mean, with your family?"

"Um, it's—hold on one second . . ." Rhyme could hear a man's voice yelling, then Birdie scraping her chair away from the table. Rhyme heard her say, "Please, can you guys not do this here?" Then some muffled, angry voices. "Hey, sorry. I had to step away from them. Texas is horrible, and it has nothing to do with Texas," she said. "It's my parents." Rhyme fell silent, hearing the worry in her friend's voice. "They'll fight about anything. Sometimes it's about money, or how to deal with my cousins. They'll even fight about what to eat for dinner. Just now? They got into a screaming match over whether or not to put sugar in their coffee."

"Oh no, Birdie . . . I'm so sorry," Rhyme said.

"It's fine, I just —I'm coming! Jeez!—Rhyme? I have to go."

"Go, go, it's fi—"

"I said, I'm *coming!*" With a click, Birdie hung up. Rhyme wondered how T. K. was handling all of this. It sounded awful. Secretly, though, Rhyme had to admit she was glad there might be another reason T. K. wasn't calling her. Even if she hated the reason itself.

Rhyme felt Reggie brush against her leg. This past week, their walks together had taken them farther and farther, traversing nearly every street in Attaway. She fastened his leash, and out they went. Past rows of cheerful clapboard houses, white and yellow and powder blue in the fading light. Up the little hill that gave way to the town, where a few cars idled outside Junior's Diner, and an elderly clerk closed up the bank. In the alley behind Allen's Arcade, Reggie's ears perked up even higher than usual—as if he knew what Rhyme was *really* after. Each night, she kept her eyes peeled for two silhouettes in the distance.

It had been over a week since the break-in at Mrs. Simpson's and the twins had vanished into thin air. Rhyme couldn't stop thinking about them. She kept seeing them out of the corner of her eye. In the library, outside the movie theater, beneath the flagpole. But when she turned to look, they were never there. Every time this happened, Rhyme said to herself, "Ha no way," the paltry text that T. K. had written last week. She still hadn't responded. Much as she tried, there seemed to be nothing to say.

As she and Reggie doubled back toward Mrs. Simpson's, Rhyme's phone buzzed in her pocket. Could it be him? She decided not to check. It was probably Harmony bragging about her latest punch line, or Ms. Sharpe telling her to come in early tomorrow. By the time she got to the front yard, Rhyme was practically sprinting.

While Reggie helped to fertilize the rosebushes, Rhyme stole a glance at her phone.

(2) New Messages from T. K.

Impatiently—and hopefully—Rhyme opened the texts. One was a snapshot of T. K. in front of the HOLLYWOOD sign and the other: "Sup, Rhyme?" *That was it?* She tried not to overreact. At least it was better than "Ha no way." But, still. The text seemed so *friendly*, so impersonal. Maybe it hadn't even been T. K.'s idea—and Birdie had put him up to it. Didn't he have so much more to tell her? Sometimes, T. K. could be such a . . . *boy*.

Reggie yelped from the base of the elm tree. He had finished doing his business and was ready to be picked up and fed. "Yeah, yeah, I'm coming," Rhyme said, pocketing her phone with disappointment. She knelt down to pick him up, stopping to scratch him behind the ears. That made him flop over to have his belly scratched. Dogs were so easy to understand. You knew exactly what they wanted and didn't want. "C'mon, boy," Rhyme said, hoisting the terrier up.

That's when she saw it: a faint, worn heart carved into the bark of the tree in front of Mrs. Simpson's. Rhyme must have passed the tree at least a thousand times before—it was a large, gnarled oak that took up most of Mrs. Simpson's front yard—but she never noticed the carving. Rhyme put Reggie back down and traced her finger along the faded grooves, a heart encircling two initials: "B. C. + V. P."

Mrs. Simpson's first name was Anne, her late husband's was Fred, and their daughter's was Leslie. Nobody with any of those initials. So whoever "B. C." and "V. P." were, she doubted they were Simpsons. Which meant it might've been carved by somebody else. Somebody who lived in the house a long time ago. As she pressed her hand to the knotted wood, Rhyme remembered Conrad's voice. . . .

 . . . *Finding out if this is really Grandma Bea's place.*

CHAPTER 7

"Here you go," Ms. Sharpe said, dropping another dusty stack in front of Rhyme. Old editions of the *Attaway Appeal*, from the sixties. "Would you be a dear and sift through these?" Ms. Sharpe often made her directives sound like favors. "Why don't we organize them chronologically and photocopy any coverage of the Attaway sit-ins? We'd be remiss not to feature the civil rights movement in our 'Through the Ages' retrospective, don't you think? But how do you choose? I mean, there's the Civil Rights Act and Voting Rights Act, obviously . . . Then there's *Brown v. Board of Education* or *Loving v. Virginia* . . . But you've studied all this in school, yes?"

"Definitely," Rhyme said. Truthfully, she didn't know much on the subject. She must not have sounded too convincing, because Ms. Sharpe launched into a whole explanation of some ancient court case. "See, back in the sixties, interracial marriage was illegal.

And there was this couple in Virginia: Richard and Mildred Loving. That was *actually* their last name, dear. Anyway, they were madly in love and petitioned the courts . . ." Rhyme knew if she didn't put an end to this soon, Ms. Sharpe would go on all afternoon. Plus, there was something else she wanted to ask.

"Hey, Ms. Sharpe," she interrupted. "Is there any way to look through the archives for a specific keyword or, I dunno, a person's name?"

Ms. Sharpe stopped talking and looked at her suspiciously. Thinking fast, Rhyme said, "I just want to make sure I can follow up on some of these leads." She pointed to the papers. "If I were to search some of the names mentioned in these stories, maybe we could find even more stories. For the retrospective, I mean." Ms. Sharpe still looked skeptical. Rhyme added, "I mean, who knows? Maybe Mildred and Richard Loving visited Attaway at some point."

That did it. Ms. Sharpe looked up excitedly. "I *knew* you wouldn't be able to resist the pull of history!" she said. Across the library, Rhyme saw Matilda purposely not watching them, her jaw clenched. "I just love the initiative you're taking, Rhyme."

Crack!

Rhyme looked up as Matilda snapped her pencil.

"Come with me," said Ms. Sharpe. Rhyme followed her to an ancient desktop computer hidden away behind the copier, in the back of the periodical room. Ms. Sharpe booted it up. "This boy doesn't get much use anymore," she said, stroking the monitor like a favorite pet. "Of course, we haven't digitized all the archives, so your search may be incomplete. But it's a fine place to start." Ms. Sharpe patted her shoulder encouragingly. "This is just perfect," she said. "After the fair, you can upload the rest of the files!"

Rhyme managed a pained smile. "Great!"

For the next hour, Rhyme sat at the old computer, transfixed. She was *sure* that "B.C." was Meg and Conrad's grandma—Grandma *Bea*. But . . . Bea *who?* On the grainy, off-white screen, the cursor blinked and blinked, as if daring Rhyme to take a guess. First she typed in "Bea." No results. "Bee," in case it was like the bug; again, nothing. *Maybe it was short for . . .* "Beatrice" brought up over two dozen results—Beatrice Gluck, class of '53; Beatrice Magoo '74; Beatrice M. Juniper '83—but nobody with a *C* last name. Stumped, Rhyme tried Mrs. Simpson's address, the initials "B.C." and variations on "V.P." None of them yielded a single helpful item.

After an hour, Rhyme took a break from her scavenger hunt. The air in the periodical room was stuffy and stale, smelling somewhere between an encyclopedia and an armpit. Fruit flies circled the trash can. Down the hall, Ms. Sharpe hummed a Broadway tune. Feeling a little faint, Rhyme lay down on the shag carpeting, and felt her eyelids flutter. She checked her phone absentmindedly: a message from dad about Harmony's day on set, and how the studio audience went wild. She scrolled down to T. K.'s messages. "Ha no way." It still stung. Her eyelids grew heavy. She heard a train rumbling, the sandy desert spreading out before her eyes, and was about to fall asleep when . . .

"Another tough day in the office, huh?" A hazy shape above Rhyme's head resolved to a scrunched-up face. Matilda, again. "If nap time is over, we actually have work to do on the retrospective."

Matilda looked over at the computer, which was displaying zero results for the search term, "Bea+1960s+Attaway+C."

"What are you looking for anyway?" Matilda asked.

"Nothing," Rhyme said, getting up and closing out her search tabs.

"Ms. Sharpe didn't seem to think so."

"Why do you care?"

"Because while you're off on some wild-goose chase," Matilda said, "I'm sorting through all the old newspapers."

Rhyme got up and retrieved the stack of papers. "Happy? I will make sure I spend the rest of the day as bored and miserable as possible."

Matilda sneered at her. "You know, some of us actually want to be here," she said.

"I do know. It's weird."

"You're *always* getting things you don't even want," Matilda snarled.

"What does that mean?" Rhyme asked. It sounded like Matilda had something specific in mind—*but what*? All this bitterness over a lousy summer job? It didn't make any sense.

"Is *this* who you're searching for?" Matilda stood over Rhyme's phone, open to her conversation with T. K. "Something to do with that boyfriend of yours?"

"That's not what I was doing," Rhyme said, grabbing her phone and flipping it over. "Plus, he's not even my boyfriend. At least, I don't think." Rhyme wasn't quite sure why she had shared this with Matilda, who was probably the least sympathetic ear.

"That's why you've been moping around all summer?" Matilda said. Rhyme looked up at her. Something in Matilda's expression conveyed genuine concern. Finally, maybe, she'd broken through.

"He went to LA for the summer and didn't even tell me until the last second," Rhyme said, Matilda regarding her curiously. "I'm all alone here."

"Oh no," Matilda said, and Rhyme agreed "yeah" before she realized Matilda was being sarcastic.

"Get a grip," Matilda said. "And I mean that sincerely. You're going to ruin your whole summer because a boy you like isn't in town?" Rhyme didn't say anything. "Lord, you set feminism back decades," Matilda said. "Betty Friedan would be so disappointed."

"What did you say?" Rhyme said, her eyes suddenly wide.

"Have you never read *The Feminine Mystique*?" Matilda scoffed. "Super famous feminist book? We've definitely come a long way since then, but I guess your gender values are more consistent with the fifties. . . ."

"Hey!" Rhyme didn't know for sure—but that sounded like an insult.

"Here," said Matilda, pulling a white hardcover book with orange lettering from a nearby shelf and handing it to Rhyme. "Why don't you give it a whirl?" Rhyme held up the book, a library copy wrapped in cellophane. On the spine, it said: THE FEMININE MYSTIQUE—FRIEDAN, B.

"Bea isn't *Bea*!" Rhyme said, standing up in place. "Bea is *B*!"

Matilda looked like she was witnessing a mental breakdown. "I don't have time for this." She sighed. "I'll be in the other room when you've come to your senses."

Rhyme raced to the computer. Her head was buzzing. For the first time since the Spring Fling, when she'd snuck into the school dance dressed in a chicken costume, she felt exhilarated. She set her fingers on the keyboard, and changed the date range to 1960–1970. In the back of her mind, she realized that even if *B* was an initial, it could stand for anything—Brenda, Barbara, Bellatrix . . . But she had a good feeling about this one. In the search window, she typed "Betty+C." Right away, a record popped up for the Attaway Horticultural Society, and four names down she found it:

BETTY CASSIDY, CLASS OF 1967

Rhyme still had no clue where the twins were hiding. But now she was one step closer to finding out who they were.

CHAPTER 8

As the sun set, Rhyme pedaled furiously around town on her single-speed bike, looking for any sign of the red station wagon. She sped to Attaway High, where Betty must have gone when she lived at Mrs. Simpson's. Maybe the twins would be breaking into the school? Was there an alarm? What if they'd been picked up by the cops?

There was no one in the parking lot when she got there, sweaty and panting. She stopped and walked her bike around the building. It was strange being at school during the summer. The breezeways seemed cavernous, the classrooms eerie. Dark windows and padlocked doors. Perfect silence. It was a ghost town, Rhyme thought, as she walked beneath the arches by the fountain. It was almost a year ago that T. K. had flagged her down after the pep rally, with something to give her. As usual, he'd come up empty-handed.

The twins weren't at Allen's Arcade, either. That place was sort of depressing now, too. Earlier that year, the girls had tried to save it from bankruptcy after Rhyme's friend Monica's grandmother passed away. But now it was owned by Robin Robbins, a music producer who acted like she was too good for Attaway—yet always seemed to lurk around town. Robin hadn't been seen in months, and good riddance. Rhyme rode on past the supermarket, the florist, and the hardware store. No station wagon. For a single day the twins had lit up her summer like fireflies, and now they were gone for good. So much for solving a mystery.

Defeated, Rhyme parked her bike outside Junior's. Most mornings, she spent her lunch money on one of Junior's famous "Oh Mama" omelettes, surrounded by old-timers from Attaway, Millwood, and sometimes as far away as Crown Lake with nothing better to do. Tonight, the café was nearly empty. Rhyme took a seat at the counter, where Junior was polishing coffee mugs.

"Want the regular?" the old man asked. "Omelette and a strawberry shake?" Rhyme nodded and smiled. Many years ago, Junior had been Attaway's star point guard on the basketball team. Now he was gray and a little hunched, but still a formidable figure. Though he was known to be gruff, he seemed to have a sweet spot for Rhyme—as if he'd known her in another lifetime. "Coming right up," Junior said, waddling away to the kitchen.

Rhyme placed her phone on the counter, staring at the dark screen face-to-face. She still hadn't replied to T. K. Last summer, the two of them had often combined allowances to sneak a grilled cheese at Junior's before dinner. Usually she only got in a single bite before he wolfed down the sandwich. By then, at least, he was too full to eat all the french fries—which Rhyme happily devoured. Back then, everything was easy and uncomplicated between them. While all of their friends were away for the summer, Rhyme and T. K. biked across town, tossed a Frisbee at Scout Field, and learned to do backflips in Rhyme's swimming pool. What could she text him now? A selfie from Junior's seemed so silly and insignificant next to the HOLLYWOOD sign. With a sigh, she put her phone away.

Rhyme pivoted on her stool to take in the scene. An older gentleman at the counter reading a book by Ernest Hemingway. A young mother, spooning baby food to her newborn at the middle booth. And over in the far corner, some unknown entity hidden behind one of Junior's oversized menus. "One shake," the old man said, as he came back through the double doors with Rhyme's pink dessert. "Don't drink it too fast or you'll get a headache," he told her, grinning ear to ear. Rhyme dunked her straw in the shake when—*ding!*—the doorbell rang, and somebody breezed behind her. Swiveling on her stool, she followed the figure out of the corner of her eye. Walking briskly to the end of the diner, he took a seat opposite the giant menu, which soon fell to the table to reveal . . .

"Meg?" Rhyme said to herself.

"What?" asked Junior.

"Nothing," she said, getting up from the counter. She padded over to the last booth, where the twins were huddled in conversation. Before she could say anything, Conrad looked up.

"You again?" He made a face—not entirely displeased, she thought. Conrad had another baseball cap pulled low over his eyes. And Meg, who finally put down her menu and acknowledged Rhyme, was wearing a scarf tied around her head.

"Me again," said Rhyme. "I come in peace." Armed with information the twins didn't yet have, Rhyme felt unusually confident. She slid into the booth beside Conrad, trying not to look directly at Meg. At either of them, really. She had forgotten how intimidating their beauty was.

"So," Rhyme said, "I found something at Mrs. Simpson's I thought you might be interested in." She waited for them to attain the proper amount of anticipation. But neither seemed to care. They always looked so cool.

"And?" Meg said impatiently.

"A heart carved into the oak tree out front." Meg and Conrad looked at each other. "With the initials B. C. Isn't that your grandmother? Betty Cassidy?"

"We never told you her last name," Meg said.

"Have you been looking into us?" Conrad added.

"And then it said 'plus V. P.,'" Rhyme finished. "I didn't recognize those initials, though. I'm not sure—"

"Vinny!" Conrad exclaimed, rifling through his bag and pulling out a letter. But Meg grabbed Conrad's arm—*hard*—and shushed him.

"Enough," Conrad said. "We're getting nowhere, and maybe this Rhyme can help us with the house and Attaway."

"I can," Rhyme said, pleased that Conrad still remembered her name. "At least I can try. But I need to know what's going on. The whole story."

"Fine," Meg said, taking the letter from her brother. "But before you read this, there are some things you need to understand first."

Rhyme settled into the booth, all ears, as Meg looked at her brother. Then, Meg took a deep breath and began their story.

CHAPTER 9

The twins were born a few years after the turn of the century, on the third day in May. The family lived in Wilmington, a coastal town in North Carolina, and died when Meg and Conrad were young. ("They were musicians," Meg said, cutting off Conrad. "But we never knew them.") Only a few weeks after the twins were born, there was a fire at one of their parents' shows in Wiki Wachee, and in the ensuing madness, both of them were trampled by the crowd. Rhyme caught Conrad giving his sister a look when she described this part, so Rhyme wasn't sure whether to believe it. Then again, she would never call someone's bluff on their parents' death—what if it *were* true?—and besides, it was a good story.

Meg and Conrad were sent four hundred miles away to Asheville, where their grandmother, Betty, lived. Betty was kind and soft-spoken, nearly seventy but with the mannerisms of a schoolgirl.

She was an experimental cook and an amateur antique appraiser. Even in those later years, she still read the *Lord of the Rings* books, and could even speak Elvish. ("*Suilad*," Conrad told Rhyme. "It means 'hello.'") Betty raised Meg and Conrad in her house, an old Catholic church that she'd remodeled, keeping all the original pews and fixtures and stained glass. Conrad's bedroom was originally a rectory, and their dining room table was a converted altar.

Talking about home, Meg and Conrad's eyes misted over, which told Rhyme that the twins weren't pulling her leg. It was clear that they loved, and deeply missed, their grandmother. When he spoke of her, Conrad's mouth upturned to a slight smile, as if he was lost in a pleasant memory. Rhyme noticed a small gap between his front teeth, which made him whistle ever so slightly. Rhyme found herself wondering what he could fit in the gap—a dime, maybe. Conrad described their home's yard full of pinwheels, dandelions, and secret hiding spots under giant oaks. He talked about Agata, the Polish pianist who lived next door and played wacky, experimental concertos that carried out the windows; and Stan and Melanie, whose seven children had all grown up and moved away.

Meg stopped Conrad there, her face darkening as she hurried him along. "Then she started forgetting things," Meg said, tossing her napkin on the table.

Conrad sighed as he recounted the first time they noticed something was wrong. Betty couldn't figure out where she put her car keys, but Conrad found them right on the hook by the door, where they always put them. Then she forgot her address, parked the car outside a house down the block, and tried to use her key in the neighbor's front door. Then there was the time she took Meg with her to go to the salon. "I have an appointment at four o'clock sharp," Betty had said, though she couldn't remember where. They drove around for over an hour, asking passersby and shop owners for directions, before Meg figured out the salon had closed fifteen years earlier.

"We told ourselves it was normal," Conrad said, slurping the dregs of his third milkshake. "That she was just getting old. But then she started getting lost."

Betty would leave the house unannounced, once at three in the morning, wearing only her nightgown. She simply wandered the streets, bewildered and anxious. Conrad and Meg would have to drive around the neighborhood, calling out her name and trespassing in backyards. Even when she wasn't lost, Betty seemed vacant and scared, a shell of the warm, quick-witted woman who'd raised them. One night, Betty escaped for hours, and that time it was the police who found her. They took her to the local hospital, where she was promptly diagnosed with Alzheimer's.

Meg gritted her teeth as she described what came next: a visit from Child Protective Services. It was about a week after they had all left the hospital, and Meg answered the door to find a woman with a clipboard. The hospital had informed her that two underage kids were in the guardianship of a woman with Alzheimer's, and she was there to check the "suitability of living."

Meg shook her head, and for the first time Rhyme could see how delicate her features were, how small she actually was. Something about the way Meg carried herself, or the intensity of her expression, made her seem larger and more imposing. Rhyme wondered how she could harness that kind of energy. She bet no one had ever called Meg a "girl next door."

"That's when Uncle Fiske showed up," Conrad said, grimacing at the mere mention of his name. "They must have called him."

"Who's Uncle Fiske?" Rhyme asked, her head spinning with names and details. "And what does 'V. P.' have to do with him?"

"We'll get there," Meg said, narrowing her eyes in Rhyme's direction.

"Just show her the letter," Conrad said. Meg looked up and down the diner, as if they were spies in a foreign land. But then she withdrew an old envelope, sliding it across the table toward Rhyme. Inside, the paper was rough and cracked. Rhyme unfolded the note.

It read:

Hidden under the canopy of this quiet oak tree, how many hours have I spent studying the delicate latticework on the side of your window? If it were the Sistine Chapel, it would not inspire any greater depth of feeling. Knowing you are only a few feet away, doing what? Listening to records, studying Latin, or—I can only hope—writing a letter to me in return.

Yours in eternity,
Vinny

CHAPTER 10

Half an hour later, Rhyme, Conrad, and Meg sat crouched in front of Mrs. Simpson's, staring silently at the carving in the tree. *B. C. + V. P.* The afternoon was fading, and fireflies were beginning to blink on the empty street. In the waning light, Conrad's olive skin gave off an otherworldly glow. "This has to be Vinny," he said finally, after inspecting the tree.

No one disagreed.

As soon as Rhyme had read about the "oak tree" and the "delicate latticework," she knew that this Vinny character was talking about the window at Mrs. Simpson's house (or, rather, the window at Betty's house, which now belonged to Mrs. Simpson). It was the only one in the house—in the neighborhood, actually—with a design that could be described as "delicate." Rhyme's mother had once called the pattern a "tracery," which she had to look up in the dictionary. *A delicate branching pattern.* From across the street, it looked sort of like vines growing over the glass. A few nights before, she had looked out that very window, tracing the dark lines as she thought about T. K. Yet another set of initials. Although whoever this "V. P." was, *he* sure knew how to write a love note. A "greater depth of feeling" was a lot more romantic than "Ha no way."

"So, now what?" Conrad asked. "It's not like we can DNA test the initials . . . Can we?"

"I still don't understand what we're trying to find," said Rhyme. It felt like she was the only person left out of an inside joke. "Who is Vinny? Where did you even get the letter?" Meg absentmindedly peeled some of the bark from the tree.

Conrad started to explain, but Meg cut him off. "It was one afternoon before Betty died," Meg said. "She invited us into her room, asked me to go to her closet to find an old-fashioned hatbox decorated with pink roses. Neither of us had seen it before. When we asked her what it was, Betty said she needed to tell us something about our past."

"We didn't know what to make of it," Conrad said. "That was only a few weeks before she died, and she hadn't been lucid for days."

"She was totally with it, Conrad," Meg insisted. "I hadn't seen her that clearheaded in years. Which is why I was so surprised when she brought up Grandpa."

Grandpa? Rhyme's eyes widened. Why hadn't they mentioned him before?

"I guess we should explain," Conrad said, sensing her confusion. "See, growing up we had only heard stories about Grandpa Al. He died way before we were born."

"Betty never really talked about him," added Meg. "But she said the box was about our grandfather. So when we opened it, we thought it would be stuff about Grandpa Al, and how they met."

Conrad smirked. "Turns out there was another guy in the picture."

"Love letters. All with the same handwriting. All of them postmarked from Attaway," said Meg. "The box was full of them."

"Whoever Vinny was—" Conrad said.

"*Is.*" Meg gave him a sharp look.

"He really loved her—like, worshipped her—when they were young," said Conrad.

"So does that mean Vinny is really your grandfather?" Rhyme was all confused. "Or was he like . . . a secret boyfriend?"

"That's what we're here to find out," said Meg, with an eye toward Mrs. Simpson's house. "Read the rest of the letters, then let's get to searching."

"Why would anything still be here, though?" Rhyme asked. "Mrs. Simpson isn't related to Betty, right?" The twins shook their heads. "So wouldn't she have just thrown anything that was left by the old owners out?"

"You'd be surprised what manages to stick around," Conrad said. "We found a load of stuff in Betty's basement that the previous owners left and Betty never bothered to throw away."

Meg huffed impatiently, "Just read the letters, and let's get going!"

Letters? Rhyme held the single envelope in her hands. As if reading her mind, Conrad unzipped his backpack and handed Rhyme a stack of papers—like she was back at the library with Ms. Sharpe. Rhyme wanted to dive in, but pouring over such intimate details in front of perfect strangers made her feel a little embarrassed.

"Go on," said Conrad. "If you're going to help us, you need to know everything."

The first few letters were about the first summer the lovebirds spent together. They met one balmy afternoon at the town pool. (*"You were on the diving board when we locked eyes, and time stood still."*) Then, when school came back in session, they danced together at the junior sock hop. (*"Pardon me, my dearest, for having two left feet."*) Another letter spoke of their first kiss, as they were leaving the Attaway Diner one night. (*"Golly, was there ketchup on my shirt?"*) Was that really how people spoke back then? Rhyme couldn't help but smile. Imagine if Betty had replied *Miss u,* and Vinny had written back *Sup?*

"You look like you're thinking about something else," said Conrad, stripping grass blades in his hands as he watched her read.

"How could you tell?" Rhyme set the letters down in front of her. A gentle breeze came around the corner, rustling the shaggy leaves overhead.

"Are you making fun of me?" Conrad asked.

"No, I'm serious!" said Rhyme.

"Admit it. You're picturing a drive-in movie with Betty and Vinny," he said with a grin. Rhyme shook her head.

"No, no. Someone else. Sorry, I mean some*thing* else. Anyway, it's not important."

"Well, good. 'Cause that's my grandma." Conrad laughed.

"*Our* grandma," Meg said, none too impressed with this line of thinking. "Can we go inside now? I'm getting cold."

They headed in. Reggie was dozing on the stairs and barely looked up as they came in. Meg looked around the foyer, as if she expected Grandma Betty to come home at any minute. "You sure the old lady won't be home anytime soon?" Meg said.

"We've got at least an hour, maybe two," Rhyme said.

With that, Meg stepped over Reggie and opened a door in the hallway. "You two start here, and I'll see what's in the basement. Let's search the place upside down," she said. "If you find anything, shout me a holler."

"Wait!" Rhyme moved toward her. "I still don't understand. What are you doing in Attaway? Do you think there's an old man named Vinny hiding somewhere underground? Because I think I would've seen him."

"It's not about Vinny," said Meg. "It's about Uncle Fiske."

Uncle Fiske?

But before she could even ask the question, Meg opened the basement door. "Conrad will fill you in," Meg said, before descending the staircase. "I'm busy."

And for the moment, Rhyme and Conrad were all alone.

CHAPTER 11

The ground floor of Mrs. Simpson's was fairly straightforward. To the left of the foyer was a dining room with a long mahogany table, wicker chairs, and a sideboard holding all sorts of candles. Behind that was the kitchen, where Rhyme had hidden from the twins on their night visit to the house. Across the way was the living room, with the comfy sofa, and behind that a dimly-lit den, used mostly for storage. Rhyme and Conrad started there. It was a cramped, dusty room, covered in tarps. "Scoot over," Rhyme said, as she fumbled at the light switch. When she flipped on the lights, Conrad was right beside her. They'd never been this close. He smelled like something familiar, something her mom cooked. Basil, mint? Whatever it was, it wasn't bad.

"Where do we start?" Conrad asked, after a moment of lingering. Beside them tavern-like lanterns hung over a pool table, which looked like it hadn't been used in years. Bamboo folding chairs gathered cobwebs in the corner, beneath a dozen bulging cardboard boxes that reminded Rhyme of the library. A single shaft of daylight cut through the room like a knife.

Rhyme sighed. "Before we keep hunting, I need to know what we're looking for. Who is your uncle, and what does he have to do with all this?"

"Quick game of Eight-ball?" Conrad said, ignoring her. He picked up a pool cue, aimed it at the red ball in the corner, and struck it too hard. The ball jumped the pool table's edge, caromed off a box of broken trophies, and clattered to the floor. "Oops . . ."

Rhyme replaced the three ball on the table. "I'm sorry, but I still don't really understand what this is all about. Attaway. Grandma Betty. Uncle Fiske. What's the connection to the guy in the letters? Even if you find this Vinny guy, why does it matter?"

Conrad stood up. "Vinny is our last and only hope. If we are really his grandchildren, then maybe there's something he can do before Uncle Fiske . . ."

"Before he what?"

"Uncle Fiske is our mother's brother." Conrad looked out the narrow window, as if he wanted to escape from whatever had happened. "Besides our mom, he was Betty's only other child. We never heard from him, until Betty was checked in to the hospital. At first, we were relieved. He seemed like a nice enough guy. That he'd fought with Grandma Betty a long time ago, but wanted to patch things up before she passed."

"That's good, right?" Rhyme said hopefully, even though Conrad's face—not to mention that he was a runaway in Attaway—suggested the opposite.

"It seemed like it. He dealt with the hospital and got child services off our back. He was handling everything, interviewing people to be Betty's night nurse." Conrad's face grew a shade darker than usual. "Or at least that's what he told us."

Leaning against the pool table, Rhyme formed a picture of Uncle Fiske in her mind: cruel, sarcastic, and sharp-tongued, like a male version of Robin Robbins.

"What we found out later was that Fiske was meeting with lawyers and tricking Betty into signing over everything to him. All of her money, the house, you name it. Not to mention, custody over us."

What?

Finally, Rhyme was starting to understand their predicament.

"And then she died," Conrad said bitterly, rubbing his eyes and looking very tired all of a sudden. "Almost everybody in Asheville came to the funeral. Meg and I read her favorite parts of *The Hobbit*. We served Sno Balls and escargot. It was so gross." Tears glinted in his eyes. "But I like to think it was everything she would've wanted."

"I'm sure it was," said Rhyme. She wasn't sure how to console Conrad—a pat on the shoulder? A hug? "It sounds perfect!" Rhyme said, wrinkling her nose at the thought of escargot. . . .

Conrad shrugged. "It's not like Fiske was going to plan the funeral. You should've seen him at the service," Conrad said. "On his phone the entire time with the lawyers. A few days later, Meg listened in on a call between Fiske and his girlfriend in Minneapolis. The long and short of it was, he's planning to take all the money and send us to foster care."

"Foster care?" Rhyme thought of Meg and Conrad as practically adults—but they were still teenagers. "He can't do that to you!"

"The problem is, he can," said Conrad. "Technically he's our next of kin." For the first time, he seemed really, truly scared. They both fell silent for a moment, imagining possibly wicked foster parents forcing the twins to do all sorts of grueling chores. Rhyme doubted that two sixteen-year-olds were in high demand. In the corner, Conrad found a corduroy teddy bear with one eye missing and held it up to the light. "Who would want us?" he asked, echoing Rhyme's thoughts.

"So now what?" Rhyme hated to be insensitive, but she still couldn't really piece it all together.

"In twenty-seven days, the estate will be settled," Conrad said grimly.

"And then?"

"Then, that's it."

"What do you mean, 'That's it'?"

"That's it for our lives. Asheville. Betty's house. Our bedrooms, friends at school. Our *everything*. Who knows if we'd even get to live in the same home?" Conrad looked at the floor, as if seeking out his sister. "Don't get me wrong. Meg drives me nuts, but it'd be . . ." His voice dropped off.

"I'm going to help you," said Rhyme resolutely, blushing as she imagined the two of them on a treasure hunt together. But then she thought of T. K. "Why don't we split up and switch floors? You stay down here, and I'll go upstairs."

CHAPTER 12

While Conrad searched the first floor, Rhyme made her way through the upstairs bedrooms. There were four, each with a particular (and slightly peculiar) theme. The first was all green. From the bedclothes to the walls and trim, every inch was forest, lime, chartreuse, and so on. Down the hall—where Rhyme was staying—was a second bedroom, covered in seashells: sand dollars, clamshells, and desiccated starfish, all stuck to the walls. The nightstand lamps were filled with black and pink sand, and the bedspread was embroidered with starfish. Sleeping there, Rhyme sometimes felt like a little mermaid.

But there was nothing to look at in these rooms aside from the spectacle. Mrs. Simpson had clearly decorated them herself—nothing from Betty Cassidy's era, decades earlier. And most of the closets were empty. Mrs. Simpson was an empty nester, and these were guest rooms. After a quick once-over, Rhyme moved on.

Mrs. Simpson's room itself was the most traditional, though that wasn't saying much. She had three life-size portraits of what appeared to be Reggie. Though, on closer inspection, Rhyme saw there were subtle differences in the white spots among the three, and as she read the inscriptions beneath, confirmed that the first two paintings depicted Reginald Fairfax I and II. Rhyme shuddered, severely hoping she wasn't going to open the closet and find two stuffed Boston terriers. Luckily, she didn't. In fact, it wasn't a closet at all—not anymore, at least. At some point Mrs. Simpson had converted the master walk-in closet to a miniature bedroom, complete with a memory foam twin bed to the side, under a gauzy canopy. The thick duvet was covered in cushions and dog toys. This was Reggie's room, Rhyme realized with a grin. Or maybe it was the reverse. Mrs. Simpson did love that dog.

Down the hall, Rhyme looked in on what must have been Mrs. Simpson's daughter's bedroom, because this one had a winter motif. Mrs. Simpson's daughter, Leslie, was an avid skier who now lived in Colorado. Snowflakes dotted the wallpaper, and the light fixtures looked like snow globes. A card sat on the white desk: "To Leslie—Congrats, grad!" In the desk's pull-out drawer, Rhyme found a graduation cap and tassel—gold, of course, Leslie being an honors student—and below that, Attaway High yearbooks from 1986 and 1987. Leslie was a junior and senior in them, with no sign of the freshman or sophomore books. Rhyme remembered hearing the Simpsons had moved to Attaway as Leslie was nearing the end of high school.

Rhyme sat down on the bed and leafed through the pages. It was uncanny how much everything was still the same: Most Likely to Succeed senior superlative, Ski Week '87, World Culture Club photos, Phoenix Fest. Rhyme turned to the class pictures, gasping when she saw Ellie's mom, aged sixteen, with the biggest teased hair Rhyme had ever seen. She giggled and snapped a photo on her phone. She *had* to show this to Ellie. A few pages down, Rhyme found Ms. Sharpe—ten years before she became Kayla's mom. She even found Roberta Roach, also known as Robin Robbins. *Ick*!

Rhyme looked up when she saw an unusual shadow on the wall. The streetlights had turned on, casting their glow through the wrought iron window. *That* window. With the "delicate lattice-work." Rhyme hadn't noticed it until now. This must have been Betty's room, too. Rhyme went to the glass and saw her own empty room across the way. She tried to imagine it, being Betty, with a suitor below writing poetry. It was tough to imagine T. K. as the stand-outside-your-window kind of guy. She wished he was down-stairs now, tossing rocks to get her attention.

Rhyme walked over to the opposite wall and, without thinking, ran her finger along the shadow's curls. *If it were the Sistine Chapel, it would not inspire any greater depth of feeling.* She sat on the floor and leaned back against the wall, falling into the spindly shadows. Knowing that Conrad was right downstairs made her feel both safe and terrified. It was like something incredible or something terrible was about to happen, and she couldn't decide which. She sighed, then gasped. Ever so slightly, the wall had given way beneath her.

Her stomach dropped. Rhyme righted herself and pressed her fingertips against the wall. *Click.* A rectangular panel sprang back, sunk into the wall and opened. It was a tiny hidden door, leading into a tiny hidden room. *That explains the pitched roof,* Rhyme thought.

Before she could second-guess herself, she crouched down and crawled inside.

Undoubtedly this was Betty's hideaway, Rhyme thought, as she passed through the narrow entrance. Her eyes took a moment to adjust to the narrow attic, barely tall enough for Rhyme to stand. Dust swirled in the air and fell at Rhyme's feet. In the middle of the room, a ratty old sheet covered something big and rectangular. *Please tell me it's not a coffin,* Rhyme thought to herself. The last thing she needed to show Meg and Conrad was a skeleton. As she neared the mysterious object, Rhyme's head started filling up with questions: *If his love for Betty was so strong, why hadn't Vinny ended up with her? Was there something in their way? Doesn't true love conquer all?* Rhyme wanted to believe that, but she feared that whatever was beneath the sheet might say otherwise.

With one quick tug, Rhyme peeled off the sheet. She shut her eyes and counted to five before opening them. "A trousseau," she mumbled, surprising herself. Her mom had one at the foot of her bed, and Rhyme always made fun of her for referring to it as her "trousseau." It was meant to hold "the dowry," her mom had explained with a dreamy smile, which meant a box of gifts from a bride to a groom. Rhyme was pretty sure this was a trousseau. Anyway, it was more than a box—and it certainly wasn't a coffin.

Opening it, in fact, she found the opposite: it was full of life. Strewn about the top were photos of a young Betty in a cheerleading costume; she was always in the back, not quite fitting in. Which made sense, given the next photo Rhyme uncovered, of Betty beaming beneath a banner that read "*LORD OF THE RINGS* FAN CLUB." The caption beneath identified her as the club's founder and president. And from the looks of it, also the club's only member. Another picture showed her with two friends: "Me, Jo & Cathy—1963." Digging around the box, Rhyme found some mismatched earrings, a stack of silver dollars, and an old piece of paper in a red sleeve.

"What is this?" Rhyme heard behind her. She jumped and clasped her chest. But it was just Conrad. "I came to see how you were doing. Nothing downstairs but old remote controls and receipts from the drugstore." He trailed off as he laid eyes on the treasure trove. "Is that . . ." he said, unable to finish. Rhyme nodded and backed up, as if to give him space with his family.

"Should I get Meg?" she asked. Conrad was silent for a moment.

"No. Don't," he said, still eyeing the trousseau. "Let's just us two look for a minute. We haven't even found anything useful. Meg will just want to get straight to business, rip this thing apart." Rhyme's heart skipped a beat. In the dark she couldn't see the expression on his face, or the tattoos on his arms, but she could feel his presence. He had a kind soul. He must have gotten that from his grandmother. *That and his bad sight*, Rhyme thought, as he cleaned his glasses on his shirt.

"Shall we?" said Conrad, as he turned on the flashlight on his cell phone. "There's gotta be years of memories in here." He held up the picture of Betty under the banner and smiled proudly. "You go here, too?" he asked Rhyme.

"Attaway High? Oh, yeah. I'll be a freshman in September," she said, immediately regretting reminding him of her age.

"I'm guessing you're a cheerleader, too," he said.

"No way! Dance team forever!" Conrad raised his eyebrows, and Rhyme laughed. "Seriously, they're way different."

"You just strike me as the all-American girl," he said. Rhyme gritted her teeth, as that was just one degree from "girl next door." But he stopped there. "You know what I mean, cheerleader with the quarterback boyfriend, probably class president."

Rhyme laughed. "I could never. The president has to give lots of speeches. Talking in front of all those people? No way." She shook her head with fearful eyes.

"I doubt that," Conrad said. "You're brave. I have the bruise to show for it." He pointed to his shin.

"Sorry about that . . ." Rhyme bit her lip.

Conrad looked through a few more items—straight-A report cards, dried-up pens, a broken protractor, a muddy copy of *To Kill a Mockingbird,* and a recipe for "Pineapple Upside Down Cake" among them—before he turned back to Rhyme. "So where are your parents, anyhow?" he said.

Rhyme hesitated. Then, she told him about her summer. Harmony's show. Her parents abandoning her. Her friends ditching her. Everything . . . with one notable exception. She never mentioned T. K. *Does it not matter, or am I hiding him on purpose?* Whatever the reason, she avoided the subject altogether. "I don't know, I just feel really alone," she said.

Conrad nodded. "I know how you feel."

"I'm sorry, I didn't even think about . . ." Rhyme wanted to bang her head against the wall. Conrad had lost both his parents and his grandmother and was on the brink of losing everything else. "My problems are nothing compared to yours," she said.

But Conrad waved her concern away. Then, after a moment, he turned to her. "You know, my parents didn't die at a concert." *Aha!* Rhyme couldn't help but smile to herself. "Meg is always making up those stories," Conrad continued. "I think it's still too painful for her to talk about, it's easier for her to lie. She's strong, and hard, but only because she has to protect so much softness inside."

Rhyme didn't say anything.

"My mom died in childbirth," he said. "So I never really knew her. We learned a lot about her from Betty, though." He pulled out his phone and showed Rhyme a picture of a framed photograph. Conrad and Meg's mother had indeed been beautiful, her skin a shade darker, and eyes even greener than theirs. To think she was even loosely connected to boring old Attaway was a credit to the town.

"She looks a lot like Meg," Rhyme said. "And you, too, obviously, being twins and all." *Shut up, Rhyme.* In awkward situations, Rhyme often became a chatterbox. Trying to change the subject, she asked, "What was your dad like?"

Conrad let out a long breath. "That one's harder, because I can remember him. It's more difficult to describe people you know. You know?" Rhyme nodded, thinking of T. K. again.

Conrad thought for a second. "My dad was half Filipino and half Japanese. Both his parents were immigrants," he began. "So, we're really a melting pot of nationalities and ethnicities." Conrad wiped some dust from the wooden rosebuds that lined the trousseau. "Especially now that we don't even know who our real grandfather is. I dunno," he said, trying to lighten the mood with a hollow laugh. "Sometimes I just feel like I'm having a bit of an identity crisis, you know? Meg, too, I think. It's the reason she's so determined to find our real grandfather."

Rhyme nodded. "I—I just want to," she stuttered, unsure of what to say. Their faces were less than a foot apart. *Is he about to? Or am I—*

"What's that?" said Conrad, nodding at the red envelope Rhyme was still holding.

"Not sure," said Rhyme, as she held it up in the wan light. But before they could investigate further, an interruption came from downstairs.

"Guys!" Meg called, her voice drawing closer. "Where are you?"

Conrad stooped back out through the door. Rhyme following behind. As she shut the panel, Conrad put a finger to his lips. They had a secret now. On the way down, Rhyme slipped the red envelope into her backpack, before hurrying to the first floor. Downstairs,

Conrad was in the process of telling Meg that their search hadn't turned up anything.

"Well that makes one of us," she said, with a slight air of superiority. "I found something in the basement—"

"What?"

"—behind the boiler," she finished, outstretching her arm and opening her palm.

"A pin?" Conrad asked, picking up the small black object. But it wasn't just a pin, and as he held it up to the light, Rhyme saw it wasn't black, either.

"It's a Purple Heart."

CHAPTER 13

Early the next morning, Rhyme arrived at the library with a lot on her mind. *And a lot in my backpack, too,* she thought, rolling her eyes. Making sure nobody was looking, she took out a list of instructions from Meg about the Purple Heart she'd found in the boiler room. Tempting as it was, Rhyme still had two math problem sets left to complete—casualties of spending all night with the twins. If she fell behind on homework, Rhyme knew that Ms. Sharpe would keep her late. As the librarian paced in and out of her storage closet, the air conditioner puttered on, the computers started humming, and $ax^2 + bz + c$ danced in front of Rhyme's eyes . . .

But try as she might to concentrate on the quadratic formula, her attention kept drifting back to the night before. Meg and Conrad had hid at Rhyme's house while Mrs. Simpson came home from the Sunset Club, all dolled up, and bragging about beating

Mr. Fitzroy in canasta. It was nearly eleven before Mrs. Simpson went to bed and Rhyme could sneak out. The twins were hard at work in the kitchen, scribbling on a pad of paper. Conrad's sleeves were rolled up to show off the inky, cryptic patterns that adorned his arms. Meg, looking puzzled, kept blowing a lock of hair from her forehead. Her phone displayed the search results for "Purple Heart": *A military decoration awarded in the name of the president to those wounded or killed while serving with the US military.*

Their working theory was that Vinny had served in the war ("Vietnam probably," Rhyme had piped up, using her recently acquired knowledge of 1960s Attaway to good use. Conrad and Meg had been impressed.) "Wounded, obviously," Meg had chimed in, since Vinny's last letter to Betty was from only five years ago. According to the twins, that meant there should be some record of enlistment, or maybe even an article about Vinny's wartime service. "You have to do this," Meg had said to Rhyme, grabbing her shoulder—almost like a friend. "We don't have access to the library."

Which was how Rhyme found herself once again hunched over the ancient computer console. It took almost ten minutes to "boot up," and still used something called a "dial-up connection," Ms. Sharpe had explained. Apparently, that meant *old and slow.* Finally, the screen snap-and-crackled to life.

Rhyme called up the search engine, and hit the clackety keys. . . .

. . . "Vinny" + "P" + "Purple Heart" . . .

. . . "Vincent" + "Purple Heart" . . .

. . . "VP" + "Purple Heart" + "injury" . . .

. . .and so on, and on, and on . . .

After an hour of scouring different names, nicknames, and permutations, Rhyme had turned up zilch. Nothing about a Purple Heart for a Vincent, Vinny, or anyone similar. Maybe it was never reported, or worse, never uploaded. Ms. Sharpe had said the library still rented several storage units filled with papers waiting to be scanned.

"Just look up 'Purple Heart recipients,'" Meg texted when Rhyme said she couldn't find anything. "How many could there possibly be?"

"Like, in the entire world?"

Meg hadn't responded. The answer was almost two million soldiers who had been wounded or killed. And that was just a rough estimate. There was no way to search beyond name, and there were over 364,000 names that included a *V.* Nine hundred eighty-four thousand if you included last names.

They weren't going to find Vinny this way. At least not today. So Rhyme moved on to mission two, which was more like a joint mission, she decided. She and Conrad had come up with it together. *She and Conrad . . .* It was an obvious idea, actually. But there was a saying about the things right in front of your nose. *Like Conrad,* Rhyme thought, and it had taken until the night before to make her think of it.

"We need to check Betty's yearbook," Rhyme had said. "Vinny must have gone to school with her." Conrad had said he didn't remember ever seeing his grandmother's yearbooks, even though they had to be somewhere in her labyrinth of an attic. Luckily, the Attaway Public Library kept copies of the high school yearbooks.

Betty was class of '67, and Rhyme flipped immediately to the back of that yearbook, following a hunch. "Best Couple." Rhyme would certainly have voted for them. But it wasn't them—it was "Allen Powell and Cathy Fitzroy." Whoever they were. *If Meg and Conrad found their real grandfather*, Rhyme suddenly wondered, *would they stay here? Would they go to Attaway High?* She couldn't imagine them fitting in. Or picture Conrad tossing a football with T. K., Flash, and Ace. For a split second, Rhyme had a crazy thought: *Best Couple: Rhyme and Conrad.*

She put the thought out of her mind. They weren't even in the same grade. Not to mention, T. K. She felt it again, that deep pit of guilt in her stomach. But she had done nothing wrong! *Right?* Was it cheating to think about someone else? Was her relationship with T. K. even serious enough that it could be considered cheating?

Rhyme flipped to the senior portraits. She found Betty quickly, since her portrait stood out from the rest. Betty looked different from Meg, even though they were clearly cut from the same cloth. Flightier, or something. Less intense. Betty looked kind, if strange. She wore white, flowing robes, her hair in braids and covered with a tall crown. And Rhyme wasn't positive, but it looked like she may have put on fake pointy ears as well.

But there was no Vinny or Vincent in Betty's year. Rhyme checked three years above and below as well. None that matched Vinny.

Yet again, she was stuck.

She dug around in her backpack for some lip gloss, and instead came up with the red envelope from the night before. With her fingernails, she opened the seal, and pulled out a single sheet of paper. Bordered by blue flowers, a gray rectangle with an eagle above it spelled out the words: "H. U. Y. Enterprises," and beneath that were a few signatures and dates. Rhyme searched for the name on her phone, and found a single entry, explaining the company had gone defunct many years ago. *Another dead end.* She was about to tidy up when another presence entered the room. Quickly, she put the stock certificate back in her bag, reminding herself to return it to the trousseau.

"You got here awfully early today," said a voice from behind her. "What's going on?"

Matilda.

CHAPTER 14

The two girls hadn't spoken in days. Not since Rhyme had misfiled Attaway's coverage of the Pentagon Papers, and Matilda had thrown a conniption. Now, she stood next to Rhyme without saying anything. Rhyme braced for impact.

"You trying to upstage me?" Matilda said, offering a weak grin. "I'll have to start coming in at six!" The only thing worse than Matilda's bad attitude was when she tried to be friendly. That almost always spelled danger. "What are you up to?"

Rhyme answered cautiously. "I'm . . . looking for a friend. Sort of. Or, looking for a friend of a friend, if that makes sense. Vincent. Or Vinny P., as he goes by sometimes."

Oof.

"You don't even know his last name?" Matilda said as she took up one of the yearbooks. Rhyme shook her head. "And you're sure he was in one of these years?"

"Yes, I know he was from here, and there's no sign of him in the yearbooks. I checked. Twice."

Matilda was silent for a moment. "What else do we know about him?"

"Just that he was about this old," Rhyme admitted. "And he was from around here."

Matilda's eyes lit up. "Follow me," she said, turning on her heel. They walked down a breezeway to the large storage closet where Ms. Sharpe kept private things—like the answers to Rhyme's homework, lots of old files, and pictures of Kayla's dad from before they were divorced. When they got to the door, Matilda pulled out a large set of bronze, jangling keys. Rhyme couldn't believe it. "Don't worry, Ms. Sharpe is meeting a donor at Junior's. She won't be back for an hour." Matilda flashed a devilish smile, and it was then that Rhyme remembered something. Last year, the *Attaway Appeal* had reported on a cheating scandal, which had turned out to be fake news. That's why Matilda was no longer the paper's editor-in-chief. Because she had stood by the story, even though it wasn't true. Principal Mathers had fired her.

Why are you helping me? The question sat on the tip of Rhyme's tongue. But when she spoke, something else came out of her mouth.

"Why do you hate me so much?"

Rhyme's question lingered in the air as the closet door opened.

Matilda turned on the lights and stopped in her tracks. She kept her back turned. "I don't hate you, Rhyme," she said. "And I'm sorry about this summer. I've been awful to you. It's just . . ." Matilda now turned and looked at Rhyme, as if trying to decide whether she could keep a secret. "Way back when, when I still worked on the paper, there was a cub reporter. He was a year younger than me. But we had—*something*. Maybe, in some ways, that's why I went after the story so hard. Because of him."

"Even though you knew it was wrong?" Rhyme stood in the doorway. "I don't understand."

"It felt like the only way to keep him interested," Matilda said, her eyes on the ground. "Because I was losing him to someone else." Matilda looked up, right into Rhyme's eyes, and everything made sense. The other day, when Matilda had said, "You're *always* getting things you don't even want." *She had been in love with Tim Sharpe*. Right when Tim had started courting Rhyme. Never mind that Rhyme was only dating Tim to make T. K. jealous. In one fell swoop, Matilda had lost the *Attaway Appeal* and Tim Sharpe. And if there was anyone to blame, she was standing right there in the closet. "But how could you have known . . ." Matilda said, shrugging her shoulders.

"I'm really sorry, Matilda," said Rhyme.

"It's not your fault," Matilda said, closing the door behind them. "Anyway, it's not very feminist for the two of us to fight over a stupid boy."

"Betty Friedan wouldn't approve," Rhyme laughed, mentally patting herself on the back for remembering the name. "Not to change the subject, but why are we in Ms. Sharpe's closet?"

"You said this Vinny fellow lived *around* here. Yesterday I was reading about redistricting, and they've moved around the lines between Attaway and Millwood about a dozen times in the last century."

Millwood. The next town over. Kids there ran in a faster circle, riding motocross bikes instead of team dancing. Rhyme thought of the Millwood cheer captain, Autumn, who had cheated at last year's competition to beat Luna and PowerSurge. Now that she thought about it, Millwood was exactly the sort of place a forbidden boyfriend might've lived in 1963. . . .

"See, the library in Millwood is scheduled for a big renovation," Matilda said, as if reading Rhyme's mind. "That big donor has been giving money to local organizations. In the meantime, Ms. Sharpe has been holding on to some of the Millwood books, especially ones that can be helpful for the county fair. And as it happens, I was filing away a few just the other day. . . ." Matilda dug around under some shelves and pulled out a stack of Millwood yearbooks. "Here," she said, pulling out the five Millwood High yearbooks from 1963–1967. Rhyme immediately began flipping through the '63 volume, scouring page by page. A few names stuck out, like Alice Hargrove with the C-minus grade point average. *At least she was beautiful*, Rhyme thought.

After a moment, she looked up at Matilda. She had the 1964 yearbook opened to the back. On it was a tidy list of names. "You never heard of an index?" Matilda said, making Rhyme grin sheepishly. "It's an easy way to find Vincent Patterson, Class of '67." Matilda, spinning back the pages, couldn't help but contain her smile.

Two of the boys on page sixty-three were in uniform. One of them, without the hint of a smile, had the good looks of a magazine model. High cheekbones, full lips. In a way, he looked a lot like Conrad. Except for one thing. Vincent Patterson was African American.

"Is this your Vinny?" Matilda asked.

CHAPTER 15

Twenty minutes later Rhyme was armed with fifteen photocopies of Vincent Patterson's senior portrait, biography, and quote—as well as a snapshot on her phone. She was sure she had found Vinny, but she was less sure how to explain her interest to Matilda, who kept asking questions as they worked the machine.

"It's just cool, I guess," Rhyme said, on her third attempt to convince Matilda she wasn't up to something mischievous. "You know that feeling? When you finally figure out a problem, or find exactly the thing you were looking for?"

Matilda was silent for a moment, and Rhyme awaited a cutting remark. "Eureka," Matilda finally said. "That's the word for it. *Eureka.*"

"Oh, right," Rhyme said, understanding. "Einstein?"

"Archimedes," Matilda corrected her. "Greek mathematician. But Einstein said it, too, maybe."

Rhyme wasn't used to Matilda second-guessing herself. But she wasn't about to complain. Just then, her phone buzzed. It was from Meg: "Kk." *That's it?* After receiving the yearbook photo of Vinny, Rhyme would've expected more from Meg. But maybe everybody was going to text like T. K. Then, three dots pulsed on her screen. "Nice work." Rhyme beamed, then caught herself as Matilda looked on.

"Let me guess, your maybe-boyfriend?"

"No," Rhyme said, pocketing her phone. "Can you do me a favor? And tell Ms. Sharpe that I came down with something?"

"You're really pushing it," said Matilda. "But just this one time, I'll play along. Tomorrow, you better tell me what's up."

Not knowing what else to do, Rhyme extended her hand, and they shook on it. Not like friends, exactly. But definitely not like enemies.

Ten minutes later, Rhyme was flying on her bike toward Mrs. Simpson's. It was high noon, and the sun beat down on her face. She couldn't help but smile. For the first time in a long time, she felt *needed*. That she was part of something. Earlier that year, when the Chicken Girls were all together, she'd felt that way constantly. She, Ellie, Quinn, and Kayla were inseparable, a unit. *We are a girl gang, like birds of a feather*, as their old song went. Over the last year, though, cracks had appeared in their friendship. Somehow, that feeling was lost. But as she pedaled faster up the hill on Huntington Avenue, Rhyme felt happy, a part of something bigger.

They'd done it. Finally, they had found Vinny. *She* had found Vinny. She couldn't wait to see Meg's and Conrad's faces. As she turned the corner, she saw Mrs. Simpson standing on the front lawn. *Oh no*, she thought. *I thought she'd be at the Sunset Club.* Rhyme tossed her bike on the sidewalk and went up to the house. Parked in the driveway, she saw an unfamiliar car, a purple sedan with the front door slightly open.

"There you are, dear!" Mrs. Simpson said, spotting Rhyme. She waved her over. Reggie sat on the stoop with his tail between his legs, oddly quiet. Through the car's windshield, Rhyme could see a take-out bag, a suitcase, and an orange pamphlet from a car rental company. "I thought you'd be at the library at this hour," said Mrs. Simpson.

Rhyme tried her best to act casual. "Ms. Sharpe let us out a little early today."

"Then this must be Rhyme." A man's voice came from inside the house, baritone and menacing. He was a big, broad-shouldered man, wearing a blue button-down shirt, black jeans, and cowboy boots. His long, auburn hair was pulled back in a sleek ponytail. Stubble covered his face.

"We've had an unexpected visitor," Mrs. Simpson said, pulling Reggie close. "Rhyme, dear, this is Mr. Quentin."

"You can call me Fiske," he said, without extending his hand.

Mrs. Simpson smiled. "Fiske here says you're acquainted with his niece and nephew?"

CHAPTER 16

"Uh . . ."

"Er . . ."

"Um . . ."

It took a few tries for Rhyme to get out the words. "No," she said eventually. "I don't know them."

"But I haven't told you who they are yet," Uncle Fiske said with an icy smile. Rhyme fell silent.

"I just mean I haven't met anyone new this summer," she said, still taking in Uncle Fiske. He was taller than Rhyme had imagined—rail thin—and he was wearing a shirt unbuttoned three below the collar, where dark hair sprouted over the silk floral. His boots were white leather. Looking at his face made a chill run down her back. While she could see a slight resemblance to the twins, the features he had—even the ones he shared with them—didn't match up. His eyes were too small, and his nose too crooked. Everything that made the twins so appealing, on him looked suspicious. *Shifty* was the word that came to mind.

"Believe it or not, Fiske's mother used to live in this very house," Mrs. Simpson said, blinking her long eyelashes. "Her name was Betty Cassidy."

Rhyme raised her eyebrows and nodded—*oh!*—as if this was news to her. Out of the corner of her eye, she saw Fiske's tongue dart between his teeth.

"My mother passed recently," Fiske said, taking a deep, melodramatic breath. Rhyme tried not to scowl. "And my dear, *dear* niece and nephew, Meg and Conrad, went missing shortly thereafter." Mrs. Simpson put a comforting hand on his back. "I don't blame them, of course," Fiske said, giving Rhyme the distinct impression that he had rehearsed this before. "My dear sister and her husband left us at such a young age. They were hardly parents to the children at all. I doubt those kids ever got over the loss."

"But why would they come all the way to Attaway, when nobody's here anymore?" Rhyme said, trying to root out Fiske's motives. "Why wouldn't they stay with you?"

A flicker of rage struck Fiske's face. But before Mrs. Simpson noticed, he collected himself and grinned. "Grief plays tricky games with us," he said. "I think they wanted to know more about their Grandma Betty. To see where they came from."

Mrs. Simpson nodded solemnly, as if she understood completely. Rhyme was watching Fiske like a hawk. He had said "where they came from." Did he know about Vinny? That they were look-ing for their real grandfather? Or did he just mean that Attaway was Betty's hometown?

"See, I was worried sick and searching everywhere for them," Fiske was explaining to Mrs. Simpson. "They're all I have left in this world. Believe it or not, I was about to alert the police, when a nice librarian by the name of Sharpe called around the house, saying a pair of teenagers who lived at our address had tried to check out books. Well, I hopped on the next plane down and asked around. Someone over at the diner recognized their picture. Said they'd been palling around with a girl, a tad younger, with long brown hair. They sent me looking at the house next door, but it was empty, all the lights off. I was about to head back to the airport, when Mrs. Simpson here pulled up. She said if you knew anything, you'd be the last person to keep a secret."

Fiske stared pointedly at Rhyme.

"It's a shame there are so many young girls with brown hair who live in Attaway," Rhyme said.

"Why don't I put on some tea?" Mrs. Simpson interjected. "After all, you've had such a long journey, Mr. Quentin."

"Thank you kindly, but I should really keep looking," Fiske said. "If I don't find them soon, I may have to think about contact-ing the police again." He shook his head as if he had no choice.

"Why's that?" Rhyme said skeptically.

"I'm sure it was an accident, but Meg and Conrad may have stumbled on something *very* valuable that belongs to me. And if it's not recovered soon, they could be charged with something pretty serious." He turned to Rhyme. "And so could anybody who aided and abetted them in the theft."

Rhyme tried not to give anything away. But she was scared. *Was he telling the truth? Something very valuable? What could he be talking about? Was it something about the letters? Or maybe something from the box upstairs? Old pictures? Those junky earrings?* There must've been something else that Betty had given the twins, something that they hadn't told her about. That made her feel angry with Conrad, that he was still keeping her in the dark.

"Here's my phone number, little lady," he said to Rhyme, handing her a business card. "If you happen to stumble on my niece and nephew, you know where to find me." Then, Fiske handed Rhyme his phone. "Why don't you store your number here, too, just in case I need to get ahold of you."

Rhyme reluctantly typed her number into Fiske's phone, her fingers shaky and palms sweaty. As he said goodbye to Mrs. Simpson—oozing with charm, of course—she slipped past them into the foyer. Inside, she let the air-conditioning cool her as she tried to settle down, taking deep breaths through her nose and exhaling through her mouth. Her mind was racing, her heart pounding. *What would they do?* If they hadn't skipped town already, Meg and Conrad needed to make a plan. They couldn't go around town looking for Vincent Patterson with Fiske on the loose.

Rhyme walked upstairs to her room and sat on the bed, among the seashells. It would've been nice to sit beside an actual ocean, far away from Fiske Quentin and his foul business. Through the window, she could still hear Fiske chitchatting with Mrs. Simpson. With a big wave—"We'll be in touch soon, I'm sure," he said— Fiske climbed into his car and sped off. Rhyme watched the taillights disappear from view as he rounded the corner and waited until she could no longer hear his engine before exhaling.

"That was a close call," a boy's voice said from beneath her. Conrad's head poked out from under the bed. "Sorry to spook you."

"Fiske can have that effect on people," Meg said as she stepped out from the closet.

"So," Rhyme said, brushing off her clothes. "What do we do now?"

"First," Meg said, "you tell us about Vincent Patterson."

CHAPTER 17

Luckily, it was masquerade night at the Sunset Club, which meant Mrs. Simpson would be out late. Even so, Rhyme brought the twins to her house. She kept the curtains closed, and the lights at a minimum, just in case Fiske was watching the house. As Conrad and Meg analyzed the photocopies of Vincent Patterson's senior portrait, Rhyme set about making them dinner. She looked in the cabinets, virtually untouched since her parents left, and found a box of linguini and an unopened jar of marinara sauce.

"This *has* to be Vinny," Conrad said, looking up. "It all fits." But Meg didn't respond. She was reading through the pages for the sixth time, this time with a red pen she'd commandeered from the den. Conrad held the paper up to the light. "He looks like me, doesn't he?"

Rhyme looked over Conrad's shoulder, even though she knew Vincent's photo by heart. Rhyme could see what he meant. Their mouths were similar shapes, and there was something familiar about the eyes. Unfortunately the photo was black and white, so it was impossible to tell if Vinny's eyes were green like the twins'. In fact, as she looked more closely, Rhyme realized it was impossible to tell very much at all.

"Meg, don't you think he looks like me?" Conrad said, trying to enlist his sister's support. But Meg, still frowning, was reluctant to give in.

"It *does* make sense," Rhyme said encouragingly. "Vincent was from Millwood, which is probably why Betty's parents tried to keep them apart."

"What's so bad about Millwood?" Meg said quickly, and Rhyme suddenly felt uneasy.

"It's just rougher than Attaway," she said, stammering slightly. "Poorer." Meg looked at Rhyme the way Matilda used to, like she had inadvertently stumbled across the stupidest thing to ever be said in the history of the English language.

"Also, he was black," Meg said in the tonal equivalent of *duh*. "If Vincent Patterson *is* Vinny, then the reason our grandmother couldn't be with him was because he was black." Rhyme thought back to the civil rights exhibit she and Matilda had been organizing, and suddenly felt very stupid for not connecting the dots.

"It's like Loving and Virginia," Rhyme said quietly, unsure of herself.

"Huh?" Conrad asked. "Trust you me, *nobody* loves Virginia—especially not with Fiske there."

"She means the Supreme Court case," Meg said approvingly. "It was in 1967, a few years after Vinny and Betty met. *Loving versus Virginia*. It made interracial marriages legal in all of the states."

"That's *totally* what I meant," said Rhyme. They all giggled.

"So maybe Betty's parents were probably racist," Conrad said, and Rhyme responded with a horrified look. "Most of the country was back then, unfortunately."

Meg pondered this for a moment. "Maybe we're getting ahead of ourselves. There's a million reasons why Betty and Vinny couldn't be together. Maybe he was from out of town, or maybe he was much older. We can't really be sure that Vincent Patterson from Millwood is our Vinny."

"Why are you so set on proving Vincent's not our grandfather?" Conrad said. "I thought you *wanted* to find him."

"I do, Conrad," Meg said. "But we only get one shot at this. What happens when we confront Vincent, find out he's not our grandfather, then he tells the cops that some runaway twins are going around Attaway acting like total maniacs?"

As the twins went back and forth, Rhyme went into the kitchen to stir the marinara. It bubbled lazily in the pot. She sprinkled a little salt and pepper on top, just like her mom had taught her. It was hard to imagine living in Attaway so many years ago. *Segregation and discrimination.* It occurred to her that, decades later, Millwood still had a bad reputation. Matilda had said the school districts were rezoned so many times because of race. *All these years later, were peo-ple in this town still prejudiced?* Her friends at school came in every color, not only black and white and Asian, but a mixture of every-thing. Just like Meg and Conrad. She continued stirring the pot, wondering how a small town like hers could've been so misguided. A boring Attaway was much better than a divided one.

She stirred the sauce once more, and went back into the dining room, where the twins were still at each other's throats.

"Love does not begin and end the way we seem to think it does," Conrad was saying. Rhyme paused. *Where have I heard that before?* "Love is a battle, love is a war; love is growing up." Though he was barely making any sense, Rhyme was hanging on Conrad's every word. His eyes shone bright and beautiful.

"What's that from?" Rhyme said.

Both twins looked up. "His senior quote . . ." Meg said. *Oh.* "We're trying to make sense of it." Rhyme picked up her phone and started typing.

"Clearly, he can write," said Conrad. "And you have to admit, it does sound a lot like the letters—"

Rhyme cut him off. She had done a quick search for the quo-tation. "It's James Baldwin," she said. "The quote, I mean. It says it's from a speech he gave." Meg looked at Conrad, as if to say: *See?*

"He's literary, then," Conrad said, not willing to yield his point. "Exactly the kind of person who might write those letters. Betty was bookish, too. They probably—"

"Have you tried to find him yet?" Meg said, ending the conversation and turning to Rhyme.

"Vincent? No," she said defensively, wondering whose side she was on. "I just ran to you guys, then found Fiske, and—"

"But you checked the Purple Heart registry, right?" Rhyme bit her lip, and Meg turned again to Conrad. "See? There are so many details we need to confirm, and—"

But Conrad was holding up his phone. "Vincent Patterson received the Purple Heart in 1972. Meg, Vincent Patterson is Vinny. He's our grandfather."

Meg looked back at him, silent. She no longer disagreed.

CHAPTER 18

"You made all this yourself?" Conrad said, heaping another scoop of pasta onto his plate.

"One jar, one box," Rhyme said. "Not that difficult."

"Well, Conrad's knowledge of cooking ends at dipping pretzels in a peanut butter jar," Meg said, and Rhyme laughed. She liked feeling like part of their team, their "gang." They were doing something important, something exciting, and Rhyme was part of that. And she had cooked them dinner to boot. *Who said thirteen was so much younger than sixteen?* For the first time, she felt like their equal.

"Okay, so Fiske said what again?" Meg said, as if an internal timer had told her they'd spent too long talking about something other than the investigation.

"Nothing, really. Just that he was looking for you guys, which you knew. And that you'd taken something very valuable from him, which

I didn't understand." Rhyme watched the twins' intently for any sign of recognition, but they looked as perplexed as she had been. "He said you could be arrested for it. Me too, apparently. For aiding and abetting."

"Gosh, I'm sorry," Conrad said, but Rhyme waved him away.

"It sounded like an empty threat. I think he was just trying to scare me or get me to scare you guys."

"*Valuable*," Meg repeated, turning over the idea.

"The money?" Conrad said dubiously.

Rhyme was confused. "What money?"

"Before she died, Betty gave us five hundred dollars," Conrad explained. "But it's already running low. That can't be what Fiske is after."

"I'm sure he spent more than that on the plane ticket over here," Meg said dismissively. "No way. That can't be it." She scraped her chair away from the table and went into the entryway, returning with her bag.

Slowly, quietly, Meg took out each letter and placed them on the table. Four in total, three of which Rhyme had already seen. She took the fourth and examined it as Meg and Conrad fought over the last piece of garlic bread.

The letter in front of Rhyme was another love letter. Another deeply romantic love letter. But it was different from the other ones. Vinny sounded resigned. Like he had given up. It sounded like he was saying goodbye.

Attaway's not the sort of place you hang around very long, he wrote. *At least if you're me.* To Rhyme, it sounded like he was trying to explain something, why he was leaving. *Maybe why he had enlisted in the army?* But the way Vinny had phrased it ("if you're me") made it sound like he was leaving town on bad terms, and with a heavy heart. He signed off, though, very much still in love. "*I love you as much as Arwen loved Aragorn, and would make the same sacrifices for you as she did for him.*" Vinny wrote. How romantic . . .

And tragic.

"It's Tolkien," Meg said, suddenly behind Rhyme. "From *Lord of the Rings*. Betty read it to us at least seventy times. Did you find anything useful?"

"Not really," Rhyme said. "I just feel so bad for them. That they never made it work, even though . . ." She shook her head. "I guess sometimes love just isn't enough."

Suddenly, Rhyme's phone rang. It was T. K.

"Who's that?" Meg asked. Rhyme paused, debating what to tell her.

"No one," she said, ignoring the call. "You guys find anything new?" Meg shook her head.

"A piece of string and a button we ignored before. Conrad thinks the answer might be in a clothes fastener, it seems."

"I'm just being thorough!" Conrad said. "Fresh eyes and all." Rhyme picked up another one of the letters, searching for clues. But nothing stuck out. Her phone buzzed again. "Missed call from T. K."

"I . . . need some air," she said suddenly, unsure of who she was addressing. "I'll . . ." but she left before finishing, the twins looking at her with confusion.

Outside was damp and muggy, the air practically rising in steam from the ground. She tried T. K. as cool wind rippled through. A storm was coming, and she could hear thunder rumbling in the distance. The phone rang once, twice. She wasn't sure what she would say to him—if she would say anything. If there was anything to say. T. K.'s actions spoke louder than words. Three rings, four. A car zoomed by on the street—gray, it looked like. Was it Fiske? Rhyme jumped as lightning lit up the sky, the lagging boom of thunder coming several seconds later. She shook her head. She was getting paranoid. Five rings, six.

"You've reached T. K. Leave a message after the—"

T. K's voicemail beeped before Rhyme could hang up. Now that he didn't answer, Rhyme wished she hadn't called back so quickly. How long had it even been? She checked her phone. T. K. called five minutes earlier. Had he really gotten so busy in *five minutes* that he couldn't answer? Even to say "call you back"? It was so frustrating. It was so T. K.

Rhyme took a deep breath as the first drop of rain landed on her shoulder. Rhyme didn't move. The rain felt good, and she had a waterproof phone case. The sky opened up, and raindrops danced on the asphalt. If this were any other summer, any other night, if her friends were over, they might have been dancing in the rain. *Dancing on the ceiling*, as they liked to say. But Rhyme didn't feel like dancing anymore. Everything was stormy.

Rhyme sat down on the curb, rainwater running over her feet and into the drain. She thought about the first time she'd met T. K.

They were just kids. It was summer then, too. Rhyme and Ellie were drawing with chalk on the sidewalk when they noticed a moving truck parked down the street. Outside, a girl with bright eyes and plenty of attitude introduced herself as Birdie. "That's my brother, T. K.," the new girl said, pointing to a boy their age on the lawn. He locked eyes with Rhyme. Later that week, she saw him again, dribbling a basketball on the corner. She sat on the stoop, just watching, until he came over and sat beside her. She offered him a chocolate-covered pretzel from her bag, and he took one, smearing chocolate all over his face as he ate it. They sat in silence, searching for something to say. Then, it started to drizzle, and T. K. said he better be going. From that moment on, a day rarely passed without them seeing each other.

. . . Until now, of course. When she got back inside, Rhyme was soaked. Conrad was asleep on the couch, snoring softly. "You go swimming?" Meg asked as Rhyme went into the laundry room to towel off.

"Caught in a storm," Rhyme said, thinking of T. K. "Conrad sure sleeps a lot, huh?"

Meg shrugged, putting down the letters she was looking through fruitlessly. "I'll wake him up. We should get going anyway."

"Go where?" Rhyme asked. "If you leave, Fiske might see. You guys should just stay here. I have plenty of room." She gestured around, and Meg nodded. "Where have you guys been staying anyway?"

"Around," Meg said vaguely, in a way that made Rhyme think *car*. "But if we could stay here, that'd be great." She paused, then said, "We're so close. I can feel it." Rhyme sat down beside her.

"I can, too," Rhyme said as Meg got up and put a blanket over her brother. Then, she stopped by the credenza in the corner, covered with framed photos of Rhyme and her family.

"These your folks?" Meg said, lifting up a photo of Rhyme smiling with her parents. She nodded. "You guys look happy." It almost sounded like an accusation. Rhyme hesitated, then joined her by the photos.

"Conrad told me about your parents. Your mom, at least. I know how important this must be to you." Meg turned on her, with a look somewhere between hurt, anger, and pity.

"Do you?" she asked, not cruelly but more exasperated. "Because we never knew our mother, and when we were only five, we watched our dad die of cancer, slowly but surely."

"He didn't tell me about your dad . . ." Rhyme said lamely. "I'm sorry."

"He never even told us he was sick. We just saw him get paler and thinner, dark circles forming around his eyes, his hair falling out as he went to the hospital more and more frequently." Meg looked over to Conrad, still sound asleep. "It's both of our first memories."

Rhyme didn't know what to say and had to swallow hard to keep from crying. Somehow, she knew Meg wouldn't appreciate tears. "Conrad took it the hardest," Meg continued. "I don't think he had any idea. He's always trusted what's told to him. He wears his heart on his sleeve, so it's easy to hurt."

They were silent, both watching the logo on Conrad's shirt rise and fall with his steady breathing. Rhyme had never experienced anything close to that, but she knew how painful it was to say good-bye to her family even for the summer, so she could only imagine. Rhyme put her hand on Meg's shoulder and squeezed.

"We'll find Vinny," Rhyme said. "I promise."

CHAPTER 19

Rhyme wanted to skip her shift at the library the next day, but Meg said she had to go. "You can't do anything out of the ordinary," she said, practically shoving Rhyme out the door. "Or Fiske will know something's up."

"I wouldn't be surprised if he tries to break in here to snoop regardless," Conrad said, looking around with a grimace.

"Must run in the family," Rhyme joked as she gathered her books. "What do we need from the library?"

"See if there's anything else on Vincent Patterson," Meg said, looking over his senior portrait again. "Now that we have a name, I mean. There must be some sort of town directory or something."

"I'll see what I can do," Rhyme said. "Just don't get caught while I'm out." She closed the door with a satisfied smile. She liked giving orders.

At the library, Ms. Sharpe was even more harried than usual. The county fair was just around the corner, and they were terribly behind schedule on the retrospective. Matilda shot a look in Rhyme's direction when they were told this, just quick enough so that Rhyme knew the delay was her fault. "We have *nothing* for Attaway in the seventies, and our eighties section is basically just a scrunchie Madonna left when she came to town."

"Madonna came to Attaway?" Rhyme and Matilda said at the same time.

"Yes!" Ms. Sharpe said, as if their surprise were insulting. "A stop on her Who's That Girl World Tour."

"How could I have missed that?" Matilda asked.

"Well, technically the concert was in Crown Lake," Ms. Sharpe said in a distinctively quieter voice. "More of a pit stop, really. I mean, she used the bathroom at Junior's." Matilda and Rhyme exchanged a furtive grin, when Rhyme suddenly had an idea.

"I'll take the Seventies!" Rhyme said quickly. Matilda and Ms. Sharpe turned to her. "For the retrospective, I mean. I can handle it."

"And do what, exactly?" Matilda said, seemingly unable to decide whether Rhyme was now a friend or enemy. Rhyme smiled confidently.

"I was thinking we could do something about Vietnam," she said. "The war and . . . and the protests here. There are still some veterans in town, I'm pretty sure." Then, she added: "Here and in

Millwood." Matilda looked askance at Rhyme, who ignored her, hoping Ms. Sharpe would take the bait.

"That's an *excellent* idea, Rhyme," Ms. Sharpe said. "Why don't you spend today gathering the relevant materials?" Hook, line, and sinker.

"I know why you volunteered for the seventies," Matilda said a little later, as Rhyme carried a box of papers back to her seat. "You're still looking for that guy." Rhyme tried to act casual, scrunching her face as though she had forgotten all about Vincent Patterson. As though Matilda had said something preposterous.

"Oh, no, that's all done," Rhyme said, unconvincingly. "Just, uh, piqued my interest."

"War buff, huh?" Matilda said skeptically, leafing through the box of papers Rhyme had brought over. Rhyme didn't respond and went over to Ms. Sharpe, who was on the phone with the bank. She was holding a check and talking about a large deposit. When she hung up, she seemed all excited, but wouldn't say why.

"I was just on the horn with the bank, finalizing the Manderley Corporation's donation," she said, putting the paper underneath a folder on her desk.

"That's wonderful!" Rhyme said, smiling ear to ear. Capitalizing on this happy interlude, she changed the subject, making sure Matilda wasn't eavesdropping. "Do you . . . Do we . . . keep any Millwood papers? I know the district was rezoned a bunch, so I just want to make sure I'm thorough." She looked up at Ms. Sharpe and smiled again, blinking her big, brown eyes. Having adults trust her was one of the perks of being the innocent girl next door.

"Of course we do!" Ms. Sharpe said. "What kind of negligent historian do you think I am? The keys are somewhere in here." She began rifling through her bag. "Wait here just a moment."

When she came back, Ms. Sharpe was carrying a stack of old CD-ROM discs, in jewel cases marked with dates.

"What's all this?" asked Rhyme.

"Archives from the *Millwood Messenger*," said Ms. Sharpe. "We had some of them digitized earlier this year. I haven't had a chance yet to upload them to the Internet, but you should be able to find what you need about the Seventies here. Off you go!" With a victorious grin, Ms. Sharpe went back to cataloging books across the room.

Rhyme inserted the disc for 1972—the year that Vinny received his medal—into one of the old computer towers. An hourglass turned on the screen for what seemed like ages. Finally, a window came up containing a dozen folders for each month of the year. *Best to start at the beginning*, Rhyme thought, as she double-clicked on January.

"And now what are you looking for?" Matilda said, walking over. Rhyme closed the folder a little too quickly.

"It's nothing, really," Rhyme said, already heading back to the table.

"Oh, okay," Matilda responded casually. "Then I guess you don't want my help searching for Vincent Patterson, right?" Matilda said. Rhyme didn't know how to respond, so Matilda rolled her eyes and grabbed the mouse. With impressive dexterity, Matilda started clicking and closing scans of the old newspapers.

"Vincent Patterson . . . Graduated Millwood '67, you can see the class picture here." She pointed to a front-page photo from 1967 showing Millwood's graduating class. Vincent was near the back, tight-lipped, only the barest of a smirk on his face. "Joined the army," Matilda continued. "Same year."

"Anything about him now?" Rhyme asked. "Like an address? It's possible he's still around here."

"Hold on, Nancy Drew," Matilda said. "There's nothing really about him for the next couple years, then . . ." She clicked on another link. "Received a Purple Heart, wow, for . . ." Her voice trailed off.

"What?" Rhyme asked, looking over her shoulder. Matilda shielded the screen, as if to protect Rhyme. Then, deciding against it, she sighed and moved back. "What?" Rhyme repeated, genuinely fearful now. Matilda didn't respond, just angled the computer toward Rhyme.

It was a newspaper article, and Rhyme read several lines before she saw what had startled Matilda. Vincent Patterson did receive a Purple Heart in 1972. But it was the next two sentences that took Rhyme by surprise: "On April 2, North Vietnamese troops attacked Camp Carroll, engaging in deadly combat that injured forty-seven soldiers and took the life of one. Vincent Arthur Patterson was a hero and he sacrificed his life in service to his country."

Rhyme's stomach dropped, and she had to reread it several times to make sure she was understanding correctly. "Sacrificed his life." *Sacrificed his life.* Vinny was dead.

CHAPTER 20

"I'm sorry for your loss," Matilda offered uncomfortably. "If it is your loss." Rhyme couldn't talk. She could barely breathe, only just regaining control of herself after the shock.

"Are you . . . Are you sure?" Rhyme croaked out. But Matilda had already found several mentions of him.

"He's buried here, in Millwood Cemetery if you . . ." But Rhyme wasn't listening, pulling her phone out of her pocket to turn it off airplane mode and text Meg. But text her what? *Oops. Vinny's dead. My bad. Sry.* Her phone buzzed with incoming messages. Most were from her mother.

"Surprise!" the first read. "We're coming home in a few days! Production's on hiatus." Rhyme took off for the exit. As if she needed any more problems, now Rhyme had nowhere for the twins to stay, in addition to breaking the news that their only hope of finding their real grandfather was dead. Literally.

"Where are you going?" Ms. Sharpe said. "Aren't we reviewing meiosis today?" Rhyme stopped, unsure what to tell Ms. Sharpe. There was a growing lump in her throat, and her face felt hot. "How's the seventies exhibit coming?" Rhyme's big, brown eyes got bigger, and Ms. Sharpe had barely uttered 'What's wrong?' before Rhyme was crying—big, fat, hot tears rolling down her cheeks.

Rhyme tried to explain, but all that came out were gargles. She wasn't even sure she could explain it to herself. She was sad about Vincent, sure, but it was more for the twins' sadness. *At what?* They'd never even known Vincent Patterson. He wasn't even their grandfather. Was she sad about their future? Rhyme wiped away her tears and shook her head.

"It's fine, I'm fine," she said. "Can I just . . . ?" She pointed outside, and Ms. Sharpe nodded, her face an odd mix of confused, horrified, and sympathetic.

Rhyme pushed open the front doors and inhaled deeply, filling her lungs with air, which smelled of geraniums and freshly cut grass. In the distance, she could hear a lawn mower going. Rhyme slowed down at the bottom of the stairs. She could feel tears coming on again.

"Hey!" she heard, as the front door opened and Matilda emerged. "What was that all about?" the older girl said. She didn't sound angry, though, more genuinely concerned.

"It's—"

"'Nothing,' I know," Matilda said, rolling her eyes. "It's clearly something, so why don't you tell me? Maybe I can help out." Rhyme hesitated, bit the edge of her lip. Meg would kill Rhyme if she told. She wasn't supposed to tell anyone, especially now that Fiske was stalking Attaway. But Matilda had already helped out, even if she didn't know what for. And Matilda could keep a secret, Rhyme thought. Like, for instance, that she wasn't always bossy and terrible.

Rhyme started walking home, seeing if Matilda, the Goody Two-shoes in all black, would leave her alone. She didn't.

"Okay," Rhyme began, taking a deep breath like Meg had done that first night. "It's a long story . . ."

To Matilda's credit, she didn't interject the entire time Rhyme was speaking, asking only an occasional follow-up. But Rhyme could see her struggling to believe the story. It was unbelievable— *sure*—but was there any real alternative? That Rhyme made up an elaborate cover story to hide a web search for a dead guy?

"So now we're back where we started, basically," Rhyme said, sighing again with despair. "Clueless and running out of time." Matilda was silent, her eyebrows knitted together in thought. They walked like this for several blocks before they were in front of Rhyme's house. Unthinkingly, Rhyme headed up the stone path, then noticed Matilda beside her. Meg would definitely not want to meet her. But Rhyme did want Matilda to see Meg and Conrad, if only to show her that the twins were real. And maybe to impress

Matilda, who always thought Rhyme was so young and dumb and silly, troubling herself about dance and best friends and T. K. But here was a real problem, one she felt sure Matilda had never solved before.

"Do you want to come inside?" Rhyme asked. Maybe she just wanted somebody else around when she broke the bad news that Vinny was long gone.

Rhyme unlocked and opened the door, holding her breath and scrunching her face as she entered. No one was home. "Hello?" Rhyme called. "Meg? Conrad?"

Rhyme looked over at Matilda and shrugged her shoulders with a grin, as if to apologize for children that were behaving badly. Matilda's face grew skeptical. Now she had to find the twins, who she felt sure were hiding. Unless they had already left. *Had Fiske come by? Had he broken in?* Without explanation, Rhyme ran to all the doors, checking to see if they were locked. She hadn't left them a set of keys.

Rhyme came back into the foyer and dialed Meg's number. She waited, hearing it ring once on her end before she heard a faint buzzing coming from somewhere near the kitchen. Rhyme motioned for Matilda to stay as she crept closer to the sound, getting to the pantry door before Meg opened it in a huff.

"*Who* is that?" she said, grabbing Rhyme's arm with more force than was necessary.

"A friend," Rhyme said decisively, wondering if she meant it. Really, Matilda was more of a prickly ally.

"Matilda," they heard, turning around as the girl in question came through the door. "And your secret's safe with me." Meg gave her a once-over, then glowered at Rhyme.

"She's helped us already," Rhyme said. "Matilda's the one who helped us find . . ." Her voice trailed off as she remembered Vincent Patterson. Meg and Conrad filled in the blank.

"So," Meg said, temporarily putting aside her ire. "Did you get an address? Where does Vincent Patterson live?"

"I, um, well, so . . ." Rhyme stammered, failing to look either Conrad or Meg in the eye.

"Millwood Cemetery," Matilda said, ushering in a seemingly permanent silence. Then, Meg and Conrad turned to Rhyme, hoping she would step in and tell them that this was just a terrible joke. "He died in the Vietnam War," Matilda added.

"It's true," Rhyme said, her voice shaky, threatening to break again. "I . . . I'm sorry, I had no idea, but—"

"How?" Conrad said. "When?"

"1972," Rhyme said. "I . . . I'm so sorry I didn't look this up earlier and—"

"And save us time, energy, and hope?" Meg asked, working herself up. She could barely even look at Rhyme as she spat out the rest: "Now we have *nothing*." The word hung in the air for several seconds before Matilda jumped in.

"It's not like she killed him," Matilda said. "Plus, if Vinny sent you the letter five years ago, then Vincent Patterson isn't Vinny, which means that your real grandfather is probably still out there."

Rhyme, even in a state of distress, still couldn't believe Matilda was now defending her. So much had changed that summer.

"You told her *everything*?!" Meg said, her green eyes now flashing with rage. She was terrifying—and almost more beautiful because of it. She turned to Conrad. "I knew we shouldn't have trusted her."

Rhyme hadn't hazarded more than a glance at Conrad, whose eyes she now met. She felt the lump in her throat drop to her stomach, and she audibly gulped to keep from crying. Conrad's expression was worse than Meg's. Not angry. Not angry at all, in fact. But stunned. Stunned and speechless and devastated. Then he looked away. Rhyme didn't think she had ever felt so ashamed. Then Meg spoke again.

"This may seem like some exciting adventure to you, something to brag about to your friends," she said, the word *friends* sounding like a slur. "But for us it's the only chance we have left. You may think Attaway is the middle of nowhere, but at least you have a family. And friends. And a future."

"Meg . . ." Conrad said weakly.

"No, Conrad," Meg said. "How hard would it have been to look it up yesterday before swearing to us he was Vinny—"

"That's not what I did," Rhyme said. "I was only trying to help."

"No wonder you failed that test," Meg muttered, barely loud enough to hear.

"Meg!" Conrad said, following his sister as she stormed out of the kitchen. "Where are you even going? We can't leave here." His voice trailed off, and it sounded like they both had gone upstairs. Rhyme groaned.

"My family's coming back tomorrow sometime. They didn't say when." she said, turning to Matilda, having forgotten about the lesser of her two problems. "How am I supposed to tell them they actually *have* to leave now? Maybe I could try to hide them? In my closet, or under the bed. I could probably feed them scraps from dinner."

"They're not dogs," Matilda said, grinning. "Though Meg seems like a real—"

"You got any better ideas?" Rhyme asked, shaking her head and sitting at the counter.

"Actually, I do," Matilda responded smugly. "They can stay with me."

CHAPTER 21

Rhyme had Matilda pull her car into their garage so the twins could exit without being seen. Probably overkill, Rhyme figured, but Uncle Fiske didn't seem like he was messing around. The twins came into the garage. Meg wouldn't so much as look her way, while Conrad offered a grin and eye roll as if to apologize for his sister, who hadn't apologized herself—let alone spoken to Rhyme. They climbed in and drove off in silence.

But they had only gone about four minutes when Matilda turned into a drive.

"This is your house?" Rhyme said. "How did I not know you lived like two houses down from Ellie?"

"Because you guys never invited me to hang out?" Matilda said, shutting Rhyme up. She walked to the front door and unlocked it, motioning inside for the twins to come. Rhyme, after a second's hesitation, followed. Even though she was pretty sure Matilda was on her side, the idea of stepping into her house still gave her the creeps.

But inside, Matilda's house looked just as normal as Rhyme's did. No shrunken heads or voodoo dolls or shrines to Betty Friedan.

"You're sure it's okay if we stay here?" Meg asked Matilda, looking around.

"Positive," Matilda said. "My parents are visiting my sister in Detroit and won't be back for two weeks."

"Two weeks," Meg repeated, her face turning dark. "More time than we have until Betty's estate is settled and everything gets handed over to Fiske." No one quite knew how to respond to that, and Rhyme dared not breathe lest she unleash the wrath of Meg Cassidy.

"You guys should be safe here," Rhyme finally said, walking over to the curtain and peeking out. "I don't think anyone followed us here."

"Thanks, Rhyme," Conrad said, looking her straight in the eye so she knew he meant it. Despite the circumstances, hearing him say her name still made Rhyme's stomach flip.

"It's no problem," Rhyme said, now idling by the door. "I should get home, though. Clean up a bit before my parents get back." Conrad nodded amiably. "And I get it, obviously, if you guys don't want my help anymore. I, um, I didn't mean to mess things up so badly."

"You didn't," Conrad said, looking significantly at Meg, who turned away. "Without your help we never would have gotten even this far." Meg stayed silent.

"Okay, well, let me know if you need anything. Matilda, you good?" Matilda gave a thumbs-up from the couch, where she had already turned the television on to *Antique Appraisers*.

"I *love* this show," Rhyme heard Conrad say as she closed the door. That Conrad could still muster enough enthusiasm for a rerun of a show for old people impressed her. More than that, actually. It moved her. This only made her feel that much worse for the situation they were in, which, as Matilda said, was *not* her fault. And yet, Rhyme couldn't help feeling responsible, if only for having delivered the message.

Rhyme took the long way to Mrs. Simpson's, walking through the path behind her house. It was so peaceful there, with the dappled shade of the trees and everything green and fresh. Cicadas whirred and crickets sang. A small creek babbled and a bullfrog croaked before Rhyme's footsteps scared it off, and she heard a *plunk* as it took refuge in the water. Rhyme sat on a fallen log and sighed. Right now, she was almost wishing for the boring summer she had wanted so desperately to escape. Where her only responsibilities were to study trigonometry and shelve books and avoid snarky comments from Matilda. When she didn't have the weight of someone else's life in her hands—two lives.

If only she could call up Ellie and tell her everything. She had no one to confide in, Matilda only just clearing the bar as a friend. It took her a second to realize she hadn't even considered calling T. K. to talk about it. *What did that mean?* Did she no longer care about his opinion? Unsure of what to think, Rhyme kept walking toward Mrs. Simpson's, passing some of her friends' houses along the way. Empty, naturally. As she continued along, skipping over cracks in the sidewalks, Rhyme noticed something strange: yellow flyers. Pinned beneath windshield wipers, sticking out of mailboxes, slipped under doormats. If this was Ms. Sharpe's big idea for promoting the county fair, she really needed to take a chill pill.

Rhyme plucked a flyer from a picket fence and stared at it for several seconds before the letters swam into order. After a moment she realized what she was looking at. It was like a notice for a missing dog, except the picture wasn't of a canine. It was of Meg and Conrad. The photograph was from a few years ago, when the twins were closer to Rhyme's age. Below, a short description made them sound like delinquent thieves, runaways with an ax to grind. And there were two numbers at the bottom, one of which she felt certain was Fiske's. The other was the Attaway police station.

Sitting on the curb, Rhyme read and reread the flyer, not believing her own eyes. Not only had Fiske alerted the cops, but he had apparently canvassed the whole town.

Meg and Conrad were sitting ducks.

CHAPTER 22

The next day, Rhyme tried to sneak out early to stop by Matilda's and warn the twins. Unfortunately, Mrs. Simpson, who had all but ignored her all summer, decided that now was the time to make up for it. After a full breakfast of all her favorites—chocolate chip pancakes, sunny-side up eggs, chilled watermelon—Rhyme said she needed to leave.

"Not to worry, dearie. I'll take you to the library," Mrs. Simpson said, refusing to take *no* for an answer. "It's right on my way to the vet. Reginald needs his paws inspected. Don't you, boy?" Reggie pressed his snout to the ground sadly.

On the way there, Rhyme kept checking her phone for a text from Meg. She texted several times, but her phone must've been turned off. And she didn't have Matilda's number. As they drove along—very, *very slowly*—Mrs. Simpson sang along to WMLD,

103.6, the local station. She remembered very few of the lyrics but belted them out nonetheless. Reggie buried his head in the back seat, while Rhyme pressed her head to the window.

Finally inside the library, Rhyme beelined for Matilda. She was sitting in front of a computer, blowing up old photos in preparation for the fair. "I'm sending these to the printer today. They should be ready by Friday, don't you think? Hey! What's wrong?" Rhyme pulled out the crumpled yellow flyer from her pocket and held it out. Matilda looked at it for several seconds before she stood up, grabbed her bag, and said, "Let's go."

"Go where?" Ms. Sharpe said, coming in with a mannequin dressed in vintage army fatigues. "Isn't this fabulous? Mr. Brody at the Millwood Home for the Elderly is letting us borrow it."

Rhyme looked at Matilda, who didn't blink an eye as she said, "We're going to scope out the fairground, find the best place for the retrospective."

They hurried out before Ms. Sharpe could approve, but Rhyme did hear as they ran out: "Don't forget our tutoring session tonight! We're a little behind!" Rhyme didn't have time to think about that. It felt so drastically unimportant, given their current predicament. As they turned the corner from the library, Rhyme ran straight into a pedestrian, knocking him over and sending papers flying.

"I'm so sorry, sir! I didn't see—" But she hadn't gotten the full sentence out before she realized the papers were yellow, and the man muttering expletives was Uncle Fiske. She immediately swallowed her apology. Uncle Fiske stood up and brushed himself off before he recognized Rhyme. His face broke into a smile that made her skin crawl.

"Well, hello again, Rhyme," he said, spitting out her name like a curse word. "Where are you off to in such a rush?" Rhyme found her throat sticking, unable to form words, and she just sputtered until Matilda picked up the slack. From Rhyme's reaction, and the yellow papers that now littered the ground, she had put two and two together.

"Preparations for the Attaway County Fair next week!" Matilda said brightly. "You should come! What's this?" She picked up a flyer and feigned ignorance. "Oh no! Are these your kids?"

"Soon to be," Fiske said with a sneer, adding under his breath: "And then soon after to be not." Rhyme glared at him, wishing she had laser vision and could burn one million holes into his shiny suit and greasy face. "You haven't seen my niece and nephew now, have you?" Matilda said no, and Uncle Fiske's lips curled into a smirk, his eyes narrowing to slits. "That's a shame," he said, looking directly at Rhyme. "I don't want anyone to get hurt." The way he said this made Rhyme feel certain the "anyone" didn't refer to the twins. He was threatening Rhyme and Matilda, who wished him luck before saying they had to leave. Fiske tidied the fallen papers in his hands and handed one to Matilda. "My number's at the bottom, if you find anything." They were already leaving when he added: "Like *Vinny*."

Rhyme's eyes grew wide and she couldn't help herself from taking the bait and looking back, effectively confirming her involvement with the twins. *Fiske knew about Vinny? How? Were there more letters?* Matilda grabbed her arm and they hurried off, Rhyme's mind racing. What did this mean? On the one hand, it meant Fiske was closer on their tail than they'd thought. On the other hand, his asking about it, and his trying so hard to track them down, meant there was truth in the story. They weren't chasing white rabbits, they were onto something real. Something that had Fiske nervous.

Rhyme and Matilda took a circuitous route back to her house, ducking into various storefronts and through lawns to make sure Fiske wasn't tracking them. Finally, they reached Matilda's block, where it was clear Fiske had already been. They could see yellow papers on windshields, and several people by their mailboxes looking at them curiously. Matilda and Rhyme looked at each other and ran inside.

"Meg? Conrad?" they shouted, panicking when they didn't immediately respond. Then, Conrad bolted down the stairs, where Rhyme pulled out the worn flyer and held it outstretched. Conrad took one look at it and the color drained from his face.

"That's not all," Rhyme said. "We ran into Fiske. He asked us about Vinny." Conrad sat down, and Rhyme was worried he might pass out. "It's okay, though. Maybe even good news, considering . . ." He looked at her helplessly. "It confirms we're on the right path. We're not just chasing a ghost."

"Also," Matilda said. "It explains what he meant by something 'very valuable,' right? He also thinks—or knows—this could mess up his chance at getting Betty's estate. Which means your shot in the dark might just hit its mark, right?" They stopped, finally, and watched Conrad process the news. He still looked piqued, as if the good news was no news at all.

"That's great, I guess," he said. "But there's another problem." He looked up, his eyes wide with worry. "Meg's gone."

CHAPTER 23

"Gone?" Rhyme said in horror. "Gone where? Her face is plastered over half the town!" Conrad held up his hands and looked at his shoes. "What happened?" Rhyme demanded. She looked to Matilda, who nudged her head in Conrad's direction.

"I got on her case about yesterday," he said, rubbing the back of his neck. He didn't look at Rhyme. "Her getting mad at you and all. But then I let it slip about the secret closet and the trunk of junk . . . that's when she really got mad." Rhyme groaned. She remembered how excited she'd been to share a secret with Conrad at the time.

"It was right when she found the Purple Heart!" he said to Matilda, as if she were a judge who needed convincing. "And nothing important came out of it—just the idea to check yearbooks. But she wasn't having it. . . ."

Rhyme knew without saying that it wasn't about the items themselves. It was that she felt betrayed by the one person who knew her better than anyone. That she wasn't the person he'd turned to with something that important. Rhyme had often felt that about T. K. Maybe it was just something with boys.

"Anyway," Conrad continued, "she locked herself in Matilda's sister's room and I haven't seen her since. I only realized she was missing about an hour ago."

"It had to have been this morning after I left," Matilda said. "I locked the house last night and made sure every door was locked again when I left this morning. I didn't give her a key, so she would've had to have left a door unlocked so she could get back in." As if all having the same thought at the same time, they went to the back door. It was unlocked.

Conrad started to put his shoes on, but Rhyme stopped him. "You can't go out there. It's too dangerous," she said. "We'll go." Both girls sprinted out the door before Conrad could say another word. They jumped into Matilda's car and started driving. First stop: Mrs. Simpson's, aka Grandma Betty's house.

"Rhyme!" Mrs. Simpson said bemusedly when she saw the girls enter the house. "What can I do for you?" She was standing in the entryway and wearing a crisp polo shirt and visor, clearly about to go out for golf. Still catching her breath, Rhyme said, "I just . . . The flyers, and all—"

"Oh, yes, I spoke to Fiske again today. Such a sweet man, I know he didn't want to have to call the police. I do hope he finds his niece and nephew." So, that meant Meg wasn't hiding out here.

"Alright, dearie . . ." Mrs. Simpson looked at Rhyme with confusion. "Well, I'm running late for nine holes at the Sunset Club," her neighbor said. "Ta-ta!"

The girls next stop was the pull off on Windchime Street, a secluded dirt road where they'd stashed the twins' large and conspicuous station wagon. Meg had the keys and might have gone to the car. She wouldn't have just left Conrad, would she? But when they got to the hiding place, she saw that Meg had not taken the car anywhere. Because there it was. Empty. Rhyme got out to get a closer look before she realized it was already being looked in on by two police officers. They noticed Rhyme before she had a chance to run away, so she acted casual and walked right up to them.

"What's going on?" she said sweetly, putting those innocent brown eyes to work.

"You don't know anything about this, do you?" one of the policemen said. Rhyme shook her head and listened to them explain that a couple runaway kids—*twins*—had been reported, and this was their car. Someone in the neighborhood had called it in, but there was no sign of the missing teens. Rhyme shook her head again, as if to say that was a shame, though she relaxed with the knowledge that Meg had not been found. Rhyme wished them luck with their search and walked away, briskly but not so fast as to arouse suspicion. Rhyme put her head down and broke into a sprint as soon as she was out of eye- and earshot.

She took a moment in the fresh air before getting back into Matilda's car. Even in the bright, open outdoors, Rhyme felt like the walls were closing in on her. *Where had Meg gone?* No matter what, she wouldn't have abandoned her brother—*right?* So, maybe they could just wait until Meg came back, Rhyme supposed. But what if someone picked her up on the way home? Rhyme had to find her, fast. There was the diner, the library, her house. Where else had the twins gone? What places did Meg even know in Attaway?

Meg was so determined to find Vinny. Maybe the most determined. It was part of why Conrad hadn't wanted to show her the secret room right away. So it made no sense that Meg would've run away. No, Meg must have had a destination in mind, something to do with the investigation. Just because her feelings were hurt didn't mean she would have thrown in the towel. But where was there to go? They'd reached the end of the line. The literal dead end.

It was then that Rhyme realized where Meg had gone. She was sure of it.

CHAPTER 24

Half an hour later, Matilda parked her car while Rhyme scoured the Millwood Cemetery, a grassy hill freckled with tombstones. If creepy, it was also hauntingly beautiful. And old. One of the ashy grey markers dated all the way back to 1810. Large magnolia and sycamore trees, nearly fossilized, shaded much of the rolling hills. Different styles of headstone and sarcophagus littered the ground irregularly, and a cracked mausoleum stood at the center of it all.

Rhyme searched for a good five minutes. She was about to give up when she heard a stirring, like a bird on a tree limb. Behind a copse of falling-down trees, a narrow headstone stood alone in the tall grass. Sitting against it was Meg. And across the way, on another tombstone, the letters read:

"Vincent Patterson 1949–1972."

"Hey," Meg said without looking up, as if she had been waiting for Rhyme the whole time. Meg's eyes looked sad, any trace of anger drained from her voice. Rhyme sat down next to her, and neither one spoke for several moments.

"So, sorry . . ." Meg finally said. She gave Rhyme a weak smile.

"No, I am." said Rhyme. "We should have told you about the room at Mrs. Simpson's. And I should have looked more into Vincent. I got your hopes up, and—"

Meg sighed heavily. "I don't know what to think anymore. We only *had* hopes because of you—even if you also dashed them," she added with a smirk. "I was just upset at the news, and I took it out on you. I do that sometimes." She picked a dandelion from the ground and began mindlessly shredding it. "And I'm sorry about the insult about the test. We wouldn't have gotten even half this far if it weren't for your smarts." That made Rhyme feel good, even if it did remind her of the looming test. "I'm just stressed out," Meg finished, lying down in the grass in defeat.

"We're going to keep looking," Rhyme said encouragingly. "This isn't over." But she didn't feel so certain anymore, which is why she didn't make any more promises about finding somebody who was buried six feet below them.

"I was just so sure it was him," Meg said, staring up at the clouds. "He *did* kind of look like Conrad." Rhyme nodded. She knew she needed to get Meg out of plain sight, but she let her lay there a few moments longer.

"I guess we should probably head back, huh?" Meg said, and Rhyme nodded again. "I saw the flyers."

"We're probably safe in Millwood," Rhyme said. "But just to be extra safe." She stood up and wiped off her jeans, extending a hand to Meg to help her up.

Rhyme looked around for Matilda, who was probably wondering where they were. But when she spotted her, not far off, she saw that Matilda wasn't looking at them—or for them. She was staring at a fixed location, and Rhyme followed her sightline to a large ash tree, where a dark figure was shaded beneath it. A man. And he was looking at them.

Rhyme gasped, tripping backward, before realizing the man wasn't Fiske. But he was definitely looking at them. Rhyme nudged Meg, nodding toward the tree and man. When Meg looked over, she saw the whites of the man's eyes as they widened. He began to retreat, falling into a shaft of sunlight. In that bright spot, they could see he was elderly, with coffee-colored skin, dark eyebrows, and a shock of white hair. And he clearly didn't want to be seen by Meg, whose face was scrunched in confusion—and with a glimmer of hope.

Vinny?

But the man was several hundred meters away, and a few moments later he had disappeared in the back seat of a large black sedan. "There's a million old people buried here," Meg said, looking over to Rhyme for confirmation. "It could be anyone. Maybe I'm losing my mind."

"You're not," Rhyme said. "Or if you are, I am, too."

They turned to find Matilda, jangling her keys. Looking out on the vast, eerie cemetery, it was hard not to feel like all hope was lost. Vinny Paterson was dead and gone, and time was running out for the twins.

CHAPTER 25

The three girls drove in silence. The plan was to drop Meg with her brother, while Rhyme and Matilda stopped Mrs. Simpson's to grab books for the Test Test. Try as they might to remain confident, all three girls were privately full of doubt. They seemed to be grasping at straws, chasing down cars and ghosts and old pins. Still, Rhyme kept going through every detail in her mind. *The letters, the tree, the hidden closet, Vinny's death* . . . She still felt—or, at least, she hoped—that something was missing. That it wasn't all for nothing.

They crossed the town limits on the way back from Millwood. "ATTAWAY—POP. 39,674." *Thirty-nine thousand six hundred seventy-four people,* Rhyme thought. *Someone had to know about Betty and Vinny.* Rhyme's thoughts drifted to her and T. K. *There's no such thing as a secret in a small town.* Still she wondered if, in sixty years, any of her friends would remember that she and T. K. had a thing, a crush, a relationship of any kind. If the Chicken Girls would be able to tell the story of how he'd surprised her after the Spring Fling, only to abandon her immediately after. If their texts were all that remained, "R. M. + T. K." wouldn't mean much to anybody. Then again, she wasn't the saddest person in the car . . .

In the back seat, Meg was clearly trying to hide the fact that she was crying. Her face was pressed to the window, but her sniffles were unmistakable.

Rhyme turned in her seat. "Are you and Conrad going to be okay?" She didn't know what else to say. She'd never seen Meg look less *Meg*. Confident, fierce, in control. But now her piercing green eyes were downturned and misty. Her delicate hands were fidgeting in her lap. She looked scared. Meg's eyes shot up when Rhyme spoke, as if she had been sound asleep. She sat up in her seat, crossed her arms, and looked directly into Rhyme's big brown eyes. *Uh-oh*, thought Rhyme. *Here we go again.*

"Why do you care?" Meg asked coolly, pretending not to notice or care as a single tear fell down her face.

Rhyme knew she shouldn't have asked. She'd finally patched things up with Meg, only to set her off again. "I don't know," Rhyme tried to find the words. "My sister and I fight all the time, but I can't imagine what I'd do if we might be separated. I mean, Harmony's just in Hollywood, and I miss her like crazy . . . Not that it's the same!" She was rambling. Rhyme took a deep breath, "I just know how much this all means to Conrad and how much he cares about you. Maybe if you just explain to him . . ." Meg lit up.

"You think I don't know how much this means to Conrad, Rhyme? He's *my* brother. You don't even know him. If you wanted a reason to flirt with Conrad you could've done it without simultaneously screwing up my life. Don't you already have a boyfriend?"

"It's complicated. That's not why . . ." Rhyme's chin started to quiver. *Don't cry, don't cry*, she thought. "I'm sorry, I just wanted to help. Obviously you know your brother better than I do. I'm really sorry. . . ."

"You already said that," Meg spat back. Now both girls were in tears.

And just like that, they were at Matilda's house. "Here," Matilda said matter-of-factly, having been quiet until now. "This is your stop."

Meg got out and slammed the door, and Matilda zoomed off before either of them could apologize. "Sometimes friends have to give friends a time-out," she told Rhyme. "And that girl needs a time-out more than Tim Sharpe needs a new haircut." Both girls burst out laughing. "Besides," said Matilda, "Meg is spiraling. You're the one helping *them*. You should be studying for the Test Test. Without you they'd still be breaking into houses in Attaway searching for some guy they didn't even know was dead. I know that she's having a hard time, but still, you can't just walk around treating people like that."

Rhyme *did* know. She almost reminded Matilda of how she used to behave in the library. Instead, she told Matilda about the time Tim Sharpe had tried to kiss her in the arcade—and she'd spit her soda directly in his face. The girls spent the rest of the drive to Rhyme's house laughing and reminiscing about Attaway. "You know," said Matilda, still chuckling, "someone should really write a book about all this."

"Maybe it should be you," laughed Rhyme, as they drew closer to her house.

Matilda was the first one to see it. Smiling as they pulled up, she turned white as a ghost. Through the windshield, they watched as a purple car peeled out of Mrs. Simpson's driveway—tires screeching something awful, as it sped down the street. An outstretched hand was pressed against the rear window, a pair of bright green eyes shining from behind. Rhyme heard herself scream, as she opened the door of Matilda's still-moving car. They stopped, and Rhyme ran as fast as she could after Fiske's car. But it was no use. The car was gone. Conrad was gone.

Teary-eyed and out of breath, Rhyme turned around to see Mrs. Simpson running (more like waddling) out of her house yelling, "Rhyme! Rhyme, dear! Rhyme, come quick!" Mrs. Simpson was in a state of confusion. By the time she'd raced back to the house, Matilda had already taken out her reporter's pad, and was jotting notes while Mrs. Simpson filled in the details.

" . . . and you know the first time he came around, that Fiske man was the picture of class! Such a gentleman. Hardly this time. No, not at all . . ."

"But what happened?" Matilda and Rhyme asked at the same time.

"Well, he pounded on the door and let himself in—if you can even imagine. I was still in my dressing gown! And he had this boy with him. A handsome young man. The greenest eyes you ever saw. . . ."

"His name is Conrad," interrupted Rhyme. "What did they want, Mrs. Simpson?"

"Well, how should I know? They barely said a word to me. I hollered after them, but they just pounded upstairs to my room . . ."

Rhyme raced past them and into the house. She could hear Mrs. Simpson calling after her, but she didn't care. When she got up to the bedroom, it was clear that Fiske had beaten her to it. The secret closet was opened, the trousseau ajar, contents strewn all over the floor. Rhyme took stock of the messy scene. Photos, report cards, recipes, silver dollars, it was all still there. Fiske had obviously gone through everything but taken nothing. Rhyme bit her bottom lip, trying not to cry again. She needed to focus. *What was Fiske after? Where was Conrad now? What if he went back for Meg?* They needed to find Meg before Fiske did.

Rhyme started throwing all of Betty's possessions back into the trousseau and slammed the lid shut. She slid the trunk back into the closet and shut the secret door before barreling downstairs and running out the door. Rhyme was trying to figure out how she would explain any of this to Mrs. Simpson. When she got outside, she heard Matilda telling Mrs. Simpson some elaborate story about a town scavenger hunt . . . clues . . . prize money, all tied up somehow in the county fair.

"Mr. Quentin must've just let his competitive side get the better of his manners. Next time you can be on our team." Matilda cocked her head and batted her eyelashes, smiling: the picture of innocence. Almost like she was doing a Rhyme impression.

"Oh, how bizarre. Well now, dear, that makes more sense. In fact, I think I remember hearing Mr. Fitzroy say something about a scavenger hunt the other day at the Sunset Club. In fact, I'm sure of it. You girls better run along if you want to win." Mrs. Simpson turned to Rhyme, seemingly oblivious to her blotchy cheeks and swollen eyes. "Dear, give your parents a call, won't you? I think I got a message they were coming home early. Tiny Harmony was doing one of those insufferable accents again, and I couldn't possibly comprehend."

"Great," said Rhyme, grabbing Matilda's hand, "will do!" The two girls walked quickly back to the car.

"A scavenger hunt? Really?" said Rhyme, getting into the car.

"It was the first thing that came to mind!" said Matilda. "What is it with these two? The minute we find one of them, the other goes missing. Come on, we need to get back to Meg. Now."

Chapter 26

They bolted into the house, shouting Meg's name. No answer.

"Hello? Hello? *Meg*!" Rhyme was terrified. If Fiske had both twins in his clutches, all hope was truly lost.

"We should never have left her alone." Matilda said breathlessly. "For all we know, Fiske picked her up while we were driving to Mrs. Simpson's. What was I thinking?"

Matilda continued calling out Meg's name, but Rhyme fell silent. She had officially reached capacity. Conrad had been kidnapped. Fiske had found the secret closet. The trousseau. The cemetery. The Test Test. Harmony, her parents. And then—as if on cue—Rhyme's phone rang.

"Is it Meg?" Matilda practically jumped her. *But, no.* It was T. K., calling from Hollywood. Matilda rolled her eyes, and ran upstairs to keep looking. *Ring. Ring. Ring.* Before she could second-guess herself, Rhyme declined the call. Right now, she had no space left in her brain for T. K. *Air.* That's what Rhyme needed. She went to the kitchen, through the sliding glass door, and stepped into the backyard. It was a trim, tidy square of grass, with a winding flagstone path that led to a little pebble garden. There was a wrought iron table and two rickety chairs. Two cell phones were placed side by side on the table, and in one of the chairs, Meg sat stock-still, staring out into the hedges.

"He has Conrad!" Rhyme squealed, as she ran to Meg. Without taking a breath, she recounted the last hour—Fiske's getaway, Conrad's capture, Mrs. Simpson's confusion. But the whole time, even after Matilda joined them, Meg was as lifeless as a statue, transfixed in her chair. Only when Rhyme mentioned Fiske by name did Meg stir at all, like she was a caged animal itching for a fight. Rhyme finally finished talking, and they waited for Meg to say something. It seemed like an eternity.

"The worst part is," Rhyme said, starting up again, "we still don't know what Fiske is looking for."

"Yes, we do." Meg turned to face them. Both girls looked back, confused.

"When I got back to the house the front door was wide open. It was clear that someone had left in a hurry. The TV was still on. The refrigerator was wide open. Conrad's phone had clearly been thrown across the room—it was lying in the corner with a cracked screen." She held out the second phone, its screen shattered. "When I unlocked it, this came up."

The beginnings of a text message. To Rhyme. Three worlds, all in caps. IT'S THE CERTIF. She didn't know whether to gasp or blush.

"You have it, right? Please, Rhyme, tell me you have it." Meg said.

"Hang on," said Matilda, running up behind them, "Am I the only one who doesn't know what's going on? What certificate?"

Meg turned to Matilda. "You know how Conrad and I got in a fight earlier?"

Matilda nodded.

"Rhyme here was keeping a secret from us. With my brother. When we went snooping through Grandma Betty's old house—"

"You mean Mrs. Simpson's?" Matilda interjected.

"Right. While I was hunting around the basement, Rhyme and my brother found a hidden room upstairs with an old trousseau—"

"What's a—" Matilda looked confused.

"It holds the dowry!" Rhyme exclaimed. Both girls gave her a look.

"Anyway," said Meg, "my dear brother and Rhyme decided to keep me in the dark about this box."

Rhyme butted in again. "There was nothing up there except old junk. Conrad didn't want you to get all worked up over nothing."

"Well, for better or worse, he didn't tell me. Until we were fighting earlier, which is why I stormed off." With that, Meg gave Rhyme a pointed look. "The problem is, the box had more than old junk." Meg held up Conrad's shattered phone, and Rhyme again read the text.

"It's the *certif*," she said aloud. "The certificate!"

"What certificate?" said Matilda.

Meg said, "There was a stock certificate, from an old company called H. U. Y. They thought it was worthless, but apparently it's not. Because Fiske isn't only here to send us to foster care. He's here because that certificate is worth a lot of money. And until it's in his hands—and we're out of his hair—he can't cash in."

Matilda looked glum. "And now Fiske has Conrad, and he has the certificate. This stinks."

The girls hadn't noticed that Rhyme had left to grab her backpack from inside the kitchen. When she came back, she set the bag on the table, shuffling between problem sets, gum wrappers, and pencil shavings. *Enough!* She turned the backpack upside down, letting everything spill out onto the table. The other girls stopped talking. *There it was.* Rhyme found the blue envelope and lifted it up into the air like a golden ticket. She pulled out the piece of paper, and there it was: ten shares of H. U. Y. Enterprises.

Meg and Matilda broke into smiles, and the three girls shared a brief, awkward hug. "Now we just need to figure out what this is worth," Meg said, "*and* get Conrad back. *And* get rid of Uncle Fiske. And *then* we're basically home free. Easy, right?"

Rhyme looked down at her phone, which had started buzzing again. *Couldn't T. K. take a hint?* Only, it wasn't from California. She read the text aloud: "Meet me under the striped tent tomorrow at the Fair. 8pm. You give me the certificate, I give you Conrad. Or else!"

The text was from Fiske.

CHAPTER 27

The Attaway County Fair was the highlight of summer for most of the town residents. The town green was covered in pinstriped tents and stalls with carnival games and stuffed animals, pens with real animals, and tables and carts selling wares from local artisans and every type of fried food imaginable. Rhyme had been going to the fair every year since she could remember. Usually, she would wake up early with Ellie and head to the diner for a stack of pancakes before being first in line when it opened. It was tradition for them to ride the Ferris wheel together and say goodbye to summer.

But the morning of that summer's opening day, Rhyme was in an empty room in the back of the library staring at a large packet of paper. Next to her lay two number-two pencils and a calculator. The clock on the wall seemed to be moving at a glacial pace, and she could've sworn the second hand was ticking toward the twelve with decreasing speed. But her nerves weren't so much for the numbers and problems ahead, but for the Test Test retake to be over, and the real challenge to begin.

"You may open your test booklet . . . now," said the proctor, a thin, wiry woman with an impassive face who looked like she wouldn't let you out to use the bathroom if you asked. Rhyme took a deep breath and opened the test packet. She had studied with Meg the night before, using flash cards Matilda had for her—and Rhyme hoped the content hadn't changed too much since then. The first section was history.

"Which of the following Supreme Court cases ruled interracial marriages legal nationwide?" Rhyme read the question several times over to make sure she hadn't misread before her face split into a grin.

Two and a half hours later, Rhyme sprinted out of the library for the green, which had transformed overnight. The late afternoon sun beat down on Rhyme as she squeezed through crowds of excited Attaway families and toward the tents near the back. The Attaway Horticultural Society had their station, a stall constructed from flowers—lines of sunflowers for the walls, creeping violets wrapping a wire frame roof, a mote of zinnias. The Historical Preservation Society was beside that stall, with several models of sites they were trying to save around town—the well from the first settlers in Attaway, the crumbling Fitzroy Manor, the remains of the rubber factory that was slated to become a museum. Rhyme smiled, wondering what would be on display, and immediately conjured a vision of Madonna's scrunchie on a marble platform in a dramatically lit glass box. *What an odd place to live*, she thought, *but what a special place, too.* A ways back, beside the Ferris wheel, was the striped tent—glinting ominously as the sun started to fall. In the back corner, in the largest tent, was the library's exhibit, which Rhyme still hadn't had a chance to see in all its glory.

When she entered the tent, walled on three sides by canvas, Rhyme nearly gasped. Every inch of it was covered, each section sorted chronologically and bleeding into the next, starting with the 1930s.

"Wow!" Rhyme said as Ms. Sharpe scurried over, flush with excitement. "This looks incredible."

"It's beautiful, isn't it?" Ms. Sharpe said, looking around with shiny eyes, as if she might cry. "And it's thanks to you and Matilda. I couldn't have done it without you girls. Now tell me, how was the Test Test?"

Rhyme shrugged noncommittally, not wanting to jinx anything by talking about it.

She looked around the tent to see if Matilda was in sight. But the only people in the tent were a mother pulling her son, who just wanted to go on the tilt-a-whirl, several older citizens reliving their golden days, and somebody wearing one of the Attaway Armadillo masks they always passed around. The three girls had arranged to meet here, but when Rhyme checked her phone, she realized she was early. She also realized that her phone was already running on low battery, and that she better conserve battery in case Meg went missing.

With nothing better to do, she began to explore the exhibit. It really was an impressive display. They had the steering wheel of the first car manufactured in Attaway—a Model T Ford assembled at the Fitzroy Auto Factory. She saw suffragettes in gorgeous hats and pins and sashes leading a rally for the right to vote (*Nineteenth amendment*, Rhyme thought automatically, still in a studious mode). They had the front pages from 1929, when the stock market crashed. Attaway had been hit hard then with the drought, the town being on the outskirts of the Dust Bowl. From there, she moved on to an exhibit of photos from World War II—factory lines of women smelting bullets and firearms and automobiles from scrap metal, taking charge of "men's jobs" while their husbands were fighting overseas. There was the civil rights section, the photos Rhyme had found of the sit-ins at the shuttered department store, and the march up Main Street.

Down the wall was an exhibit on Vietnam, surrounding the vintage army fatigues Ms. Sharpe had found. Rhyme went over to the wall of fallen heroes—*her idea*!—a list of locals who had been lost in war. She quickly found Vincent Patterson, with a "DIA" next to his name. She ran her finger over his name, remembering how just a week before they'd been sure he was *their* Vinny.

"It's time," said a muffled voice from behind her. Turning, Rhyme saw it was the person in the Armadillo mask. *Fiske?* Before she could step back, Meg lifted the mask from her face, revealing a cheeky grin. "Just to be extra safe," Meg said. Beside her, Matilda removed a Millwood Muskrat mask, and the three girls were back together. "All for one, one for all," Meg said, huddling close.

They paused at the veterans' wall, seeing Vincent Patterson's name.

"Whether or not it's Vinny," said Rhyme, "we're going to find your grandfather."

They stepped outside, and the fair was brimming with families and faces—some she knew, and some she didn't. The whole town had come out. Scarlet and cream-colored lights blazed across the fairgrounds, over the booths and tents and children, all of Rhyme's neighbors. Everyone except her parent and Harmony. Except the Chicken Girls. But she wasn't on her own. The girls stood together, three in a row. A searchlight atop the Ferris wheel pointed directly to the shadowy corner where the striped tent was raised. They started off together, ready or not, to confront Uncle Fiske.

CHAPTER 28

Tap, tap, tap.

From behind them came the thunderous tap of a microphone, broadcasted across the field. Rhyme turned to see as Principal Mathers stepped up to the podium. "Greetings, Attaway!" he said. "As many of you know, I had my wisdom teeth out last semester, but I'm happy to be returning to school this year. I trust you all enjoyed working with Principal Journey, however." Meg tugged on Rhyme's sleeve, pulling her back toward the striped tent. Everyone else, however, was moving toward the stage, the three girls swimming like minnows against a thick current. The cheerleading captain from Millwood, a bossy girl named Autumn, brushed past Rhyme without so much as looking up. "Hurry!" said Meg. "If Fiske thinks we're not coming, he may try to hurt Conrad."

" . . . And without further ado," Principal Mathers was saying, "please welcome Debra Sharpe, our town historian, to the stage." The microphone screeched over scattered applause. As much as Rhyme wanted to turn around, the girls continued their steady march.

"Wow, it is wonderful seeing so many familiar faces out there," she said. "So many of you donated to the library's fund this year— and your attendance here will help further fund our community of libraries. Reading. Is. Everything." That didn't draw too many claps—especially out here, where the crowd had thinned. The girls were only twenty paces from the striped tent now.

"What now?" said Matilda, looking from side to side.

"Now, we go get my brother back," Meg said.

But before they could get anywhere, two kids from school stood in their way.

"Matilda?" said one of them, a jovial, sandy-haired guy. Beside him was a girl from school named Holly. "Long time, no see! How's your summer been?" asked the boy.

"Oh, hi, Billy," said Matilda. "The thing is, we're sort of busy right now, and—"

But her plea fell on deaf ears. Without catching a breath, Billy started recounting his entire summer: a tag football league, his family's trip to Washington DC, how his neighbor had sprained her wrist, and what subjects Billy was taking next year.

Agitated, Rhyme turned back toward the stage, where Ms. Sharpe was still speaking. "Now," the historian was saying, "I would like to introduce someone who's been a patron and friend of the library for decades." Rhyme's eyes were suddenly drawn to the curlicue logos that decorated the tents. The same logo was emblazoned in signs across the fair's enclosure. Now that she noticed it, the symbol was everywhere. The letters connected and looped in such a way that it appeared as a design first, a word second. "And this year," said Ms. Sharpe, "thanks to an extra special donation, we've doubled our operating budget for the next *ten years* . . ."

" . . .I'm thinking earth sciences, but my mom wants me to do biology . . ." Billy was saying.

" . . . I'm sure you are all familiar with his name, as his company has sponsored several philanthropic organizations over the years," said Ms. Sharpe.

" . . . We really need to be going now, Billy," Matilda said.

Rhyme's head was swimming.

" . . . So I hope you'll please help me in presenting Silas Manderley with our Attaway Altruist Award," Ms. Sharpe said, to resounding applause.

That's what the letters said, stenciled on the tents. *Manderley.* Rhyme scrunched up her nose. *Where have I heard that before?* But she couldn't quite remember. With the aid of a cane, an old man mounted the stage. Even in the fading light, Rhyme recognized him right away. She tapped on Meg's shoulder and pointed to the stage.

Billy, meanwhile, was still rambling on. "Holly here's been doing a bang-up job, but we definitely miss you at the paper. If you ever want to come back, you know . . ." But Matilda was no longer listening. She was looking in the same direction as Rhyme and

Meg: at the podium. The elderly man on stage—the wealthy donor, Silas Manderley—was the same man they'd seen at the Millwood Cemetery.

"Thank you, Ms. Sharpe," he began, his voice hoarse with age and weariness. "And thank you, Attaway. This was a difficult year," the old man started to say. The girls all looked at each other, hovering on the edge of a revelation. But before they could speak, Billy interjected yet again.

"There's a man over there who seems to be looking your way," he said. "You know him?"

They turned. In the doorway to the striped tent, Fiske Quentin was waiting impatiently. He drew his finger across his neck. *Or else.* Beside him, disguised by the tent's flap, drawn in crimson and cream, was somebody else.

CHAPTER 29

Because this year was chock full of history, overflow from the main
tent had been housed in this smaller section. It was a tent from
many years ago, striped in Attaway colors: crimson and cream. By
the time the girls made their way inside, Fiske and Conrad had
disappeared. A few visitors and a security guard milled about the
perimeter, more interested in the proceedings outside than what
adorned the tent's walls. The girls fanned out, trying to find Fiske.

Oh, Rhyme thought to herself. This was the retrospective. The
project she and Matilda had poured so much time into this summer.
She drew closer to the walls, suddenly—and genuinely—interested.
This was the town she'd lived in since she was born. At each decade,
the exhibit included a photo of the town square Rhyme knew so well.
She saw roads change from dirt to cobbled to paved, the vehicles from
wagons to streetcars to cars. And then she got to the exhibit on the

rubber factory fire, which she remembered Matilda mentioning early in the summer, before they were friends. *If they were friends, now.* Matilda was right, it *was* a crazy story: two women had died in a terrible fire, and for ten years the wrong man was blamed. Matilda had set the section up so the two stories were side by side—the initial one, and then the truth, which came out ten years later at the first "Phoenix Fest," which the town still celebrated. One of the girls, wearing orange cat-eye glasses and a hunter's hat, looked a little like Rhyme.

"*Psst*," Matilda called from across the room. Rhyme and Meg followed her gaze to the back of the tent, where Fiske was curling his bony finger, motioning for them to follow him outside.

The striped tent abutted the end of the fairgrounds, where a dense forest rose above the faraway din of the crowd. Between the tent and the trees was a narrow lip of tall grass. There, the girls found Fiske, leaning against a tree with a malicious look on his face. He wore a sharkskin suit, a black turtleneck, and bulky sneakers. This time his hair wasn't pulled back. Electrical wires ran around the tent, and Fiske yanked one out—cutting the audio on the speaker above. Sitting beside the speaker was someone who appeared to be Conrad, though his face was obscured by an Attaway Armadillo mask. When his uncle peeled it off, the girls saw that Conrad was blindfolded, and his mouth taped shut.

"Ladies," hissed Fiske, menacing in the moonlight. "It's such a pleasure to see you all again." A creepy smile spread across his face.

Rhyme's butterflies turned to nausea at the sight of his teeth. Meg didn't respond. Her eyes were locked on Conrad. His hair was rumpled and clothing wrinkled, and now they saw his leg was tied to one of the tent's iron stakes.

Rhyme had the envelope in her shaking hand. Her eyes kept darting between Fiske and the twins, terrified that at any second he'd take them both away again. She grabbed Meg's hand, instinctively. To her surprise, Meg squeezed back.

"No need for this to take up any more of my time," said Fiske, still smiling. "I'll just take that. . . ."

He reached for the certificate, but Rhyme pulled back.

"Hey!" she said, addressing him directly for the first time. "Untie Conrad first." Rhyme's voice sounded bold and confident, belying how terrified she really was.

"That's rich." Fiske snorted. "I don't think so. You seem to be forgetting who holds all the cards here." Fiske pulled back his jacket to reveal a knife tucked into a holster on his hip. Matilda gasped. Rhyme took a step backwards when she saw the knife, but Meg stepped toward him, pulling Rhyme closer to Fiske and Conrad.

"No more stalling!" Fiske snarled. He was growing impatient. "First things first. Come say hi to your uncle, Meg." When she didn't comply, he pulled back his jacket again, showing the knife. She relented.

"What are you going to do to me?" said Meg.

"I hate to keep twins apart," Fiske said, as he sat Meg down beside her brother. "This will only take a second," he hissed, as he took another piece of rope from the ground and tied Meg's hands together and to another stake in the ground. "That should keep you out of my way."

"You next," he said to Matilda, who recoiled with fear. "I wasn't expecting another twerp, but we can't have you causing any trouble." Fiske was still holding his jacket open, and so Matilda sat down beside the twins, and watched helplessly as Fiske tied her hands as well. Now it was just Rhyme. Fiske eyed her. "Hand it over. Now."

"*Nuhhhhh*," Conrad tried protesting from beneath the tape.

"Oh, did my dear nephew have something to say?" With a single pull, Fiske ripped the tape from Conrad's face, leaving a fresh red mark around his lips. "Go on then," said Fiske.

"Don't give it to him, Rhyme!" Conrad said, wincing from the pain. "It's our money, Meg! It's Betty's money! She wouldn't want a penny going to this monster."

"If I give you the certificate, will you leave and let them go?" Rhyme asked.

"You have my word," said Fiske.

Rhyme held out the envelope, and Fiske snatched it from her grasp. He held it up to the spotlight, turned it over several times and inspected each corner and read the copy. When he started sniffing it, Rhyme interjected.

"It's real, you creep! Get out of here, and let the kids go!"

Fiske looked at Rhyme and chuckled. He pointed one of his long fingers at her, shaking it as he laughed.

"More than meets the eye when it comes to little Miss Rhyme . . ."

"Just take the money and go," Conrad practically spat at Fiske.

"You think I want to spend another second in this backwater town?" Fiske laughed, a throaty, sinister cackle. "Now that I've got the money, you kids should enjoy your silly fair."

"What money?" Matilda piped up. "We looked all over the Internet for this H. U. Y. company, and it doesn't exist. How are ten measly shares going to get you anywhere?"

Fiske glowered at her. "Maybe you should play closer attention." He winked at Meg, sending a chill down all of their spines. Then, he plugged the loose speaker wire back into the jack and yanked down one of the tent's flaps, so they could see the podium from a distance. "Pay attention, girls," he said. "A bit of family history before we part ways for good."

After a bit of static, the speaker came to life. "Before concluding my remarks, I wanted to add one more thing. It's on a personal note." The old man was still on stage, accepting his award. "I'm getting old, if you haven't noticed," Manderley said, eliciting an appreciative chuckle from the crowd. "And when you're my age you start to look back at your life, wonder what you've done, all you've accomplished, but more so who you have loved . . ."

As they all listened to the speaker, Rhyme edged closer to where Conrad was bound to the stake. " . . . This year I lost someone quite important to me," Manderley went on, "though I hadn't seen her in over forty years."

Now, Rhyme was only vaguely hearing the words, her hot pink shoe drawing ever closer to Conrad. " . . . She moved away from

Attaway many years ago, but Betty Cassidy was one of the finest women this town ever produced. She was the love of my life."

"What?" said Meg.

Fiske turned toward the crowd, which had fallen silent. "Just pay attention, missy." With a rictus grin stuck on his face, he turned back toward the crowd. "You'll see."

"To make a long story short," Manderley said, "I was a black boy in Attaway, in love with a white girl. That made her parents none too pleased. And after a few years of heartache and disappointment, I shipped off to Vietnam, 143rd Division. My best friend was a feller by the name of Silas Manderley. We were going to make it through 'Nam and start a business together back home. A few weeks before our tour ended, the Easter attack started. Three days of heavy artillery. I took a bullet in the leg. But poor Silas wasn't so lucky. He was hit by a bomb. When I made it a home six months later, I started that company, and named it in Silas's honor. And after a little while, that black boy from Millwood—his name, sorry *my* name, was Vincent Patterson—was reborn as Silas Manderley."

Even from this far away, Rhyme could hear the crowd's gasps. Attaway was a sleepy place, and this was juicy stuff. Her foot, meanwhile, had almost worked the rope tying Conrad's hands over the spike in the ground. *Just one more kick. . . .*

Manderley, when he started speaking again, sounded choked up. "I never got to see Betty again, but we exchanged some letters over the years. One of the things I learned was that we had a child together. A baby girl. Sadly, I never got to meet her, either. But I'm hoping to meet her children. Twins, I'm told. If you're out there—and you want to meet—I hope you'll come find me tonight. I'll be waiting by the Ferris wheel."

And with that, Silas Manderley left the stage. The audience didn't know what to do. Neither did Meg, who seemed stunned. Fiske turned to the three girls, grinning wildly. "You know how much a share of Manderley's company is worth today?" He held up the certificate, showing one hundred shares. "Ten thousand dollars apiece. I'm a millionaire!"

"Then you better hand it over now," said Conrad, his fists untied, circling like a boxer.

CHAPTER 30

The next few moments were a blur of blows and insults. Conrad got the first punch in, but Fiske retaliated violently, throwing his nephew against the tent. Back and forth, they traded nasty shoves, until they were grappling in the grass. "Ow!" Rhyme heard Fiske scream, as Meg used her free foot to stamp on his hand. But the pain only seemed to embolden him, and he shouldered Conrad to the side, where Meg and Matilda were still held captive.

That's when Rhyme saw it: the certificate, lying a few feet away on the ground. Without a second's thought, she bolted toward the paper, grabbed it, and flew into the tent. It was deserted now, every-one having abandoned the exhibits for the fairgrounds. Behind her, Rhyme heard loud crashes and thumps—no doubt, her summer's hard work being thrown to the wayside. Chancing a look over her shoulder, Rhyme saw that Fiske wasn't far behind her, with Conrad at his heels. With a *whoosh*, she escaped the tent and was out in the open.

All around her, the county fair was coming back to life. During the presentation, all of the rides had been switched off, the food vendors closed. Now, however, the whole operation was heaving back to life, like a giant monster rousing after a long night's sleep. Up ahead, the Ferris wheel groaned, its cars gently swaying as the attraction came back to life. *There*, she thought. Fast on her feet, Rhyme bolted ahead.

"Stop that girl!" she heard Fiske yelling behind her. It was getting harder and harder to keep pace, with more of the fairgoers spreading out over the grounds, eager to be entertained after Silas Manderley's long speech. She'd never run so fast in her life. Billy and Holly stood in her path, and she leaped between them like a gazelle. Fiske must not have been so graceful; from behind her, Rhyme heard Billy scream, "Ow! Watch it, buddy! That's my toe!"

She was at the Ferris wheel now. A small line formed along the railing. Mostly kids and parents, but there was Junior from the coffee shop. "Get off me!" she heard, and turned to see that Conrad had caught up to Fiske, the two of them tussling by the railing. "Now, now, everyone will get a turn," Junior was admonishing them. Not knowing what else to do, Rhyme hopped the fence and jumped onto the platform, where an elderly operator was collecting tickets. Just then, one of the red cars swung to a stop. "You're caught now!" Fiske was screaming at her back. There was nowhere to go . . . but up. As the car lurched to a start, Rhyme took a seat. And then it was up, up and away. . . .

Lurching skyward, Rhyme felt dizzy. She put her head in her hands, trying to catch her breath. After a few seconds, she looked up and out at the county fair. Across the grassy field was a constellation of lights, a throng of people growing more miniature by the second. The main tent looked no bigger than Reggie's mattress. Directly below—though she hated to look down—Rhyme saw Matilda and Meg crowding around the operator, gesticulating wildly. *But where was Fiske? And where was Conrad?* And that's when she saw them, one car down, staring directly up at her. They were sitting together on the bench like old friends, Fiske looking maniacal, and Conrad uncomfortable. It was then she saw a glint of light, and realized that Fiske was holding his knife right up against his nephew. "You just wait right there, little lady," he called out—loud enough for Rhyme to hear, but not for the people on the ground. "I'm going to get you."

The wheel kept on turning, and Rhyme was lifted higher and higher. Too scared to look down, and too dizzy to look up, she stared straight ahead—out over the trees and into the night sky. A few low, gauzy clouds sat on the horizon, and behind them three bright white stars made up a perfect triangle. The car continued lurching upward, and Rhyme felt completely helpless, marooned all alone. And it was then that her phone rang. *Who else?*

Incoming call from . . .

"T. K.?" She tried sounding nonchalant, like she wasn't fifty feet in the air, with a greedy madman not far behind her, and her phone about to die. "It's not really a good time right now. I'm sorry that I missed your call earlier. Everything all right?"

"Sup, Rhyme?" Somehow, T. K. sounded different, older maybe. "Just was hanging out with Flash and a few friends, and was thinking of you. I'm coming home in a few days. I guess we haven't talked much. I've had some family stuff going on. Maybe Birdie told you about it."

"She just said your parents were fighting," Rhyme said. "Is there anything I can do?"

"Nah," said T. K. "Hey, where are you anyway? Sounds pretty windy for Attaway."

"Oh, it's just the air conditioner," Rhyme said, as her car swung in the wind.

"Anyways, nothing important. Just wanted to make sure you were having a good summer."

Below, Rhyme heard a *clang*, and when she peered down, she saw Fiske was now standing up in his car, brandishing the knife in Conrad's direction. "Summer? It's, uh—It's been uneventful," she said into the phone.

"You sound kinda distracted," T. K. said. "Should I try you later?"

Rhyme's phone gave off a last gurgle, her battery at one percent. "I want to tell you something, T. K.," she said, holding her phone close to her face. "No matter what happens, I'm really glad you were my first kiss."

Before he could respond, she hung up. A few seconds later, her phone went black. Now she was truly by herself. Little by little, the car drew closer to the top, nothing separating her from the inky sky. *Don't look down . . . don't look down . . . don't look down . . .* She looked down. It was like being on an airplane, when the people melt away, and all you can see are parking lots, baseball diamonds, and tiny square plots of land. "Don't do it, Rhyme!" Conrad yelled up from down below. When she looked down, she saw that Fiske had him up against the car's edge, his arms in a vise-like grip.

"Please! You don't need to hurt him!" Rhyme screamed.

Fiske was no more than ten feet below. "Here's how this is going to work," he yelled up. "Your friend Conrad here is going to climb out of the car, and you're going to give him the certificate. Then, when we get to the bottom, you're both going to make like everything's fine. The three of us will walk to my car and then scram. *Capisce?*"

"What if he falls?" Rhyme called down.

"Then I'll come get it myself," Fiske growled.

And with that, Fiske pushed Conrad to the edge of the car. Holding the long, blue spoke, Conrad stood up on the edge of the car, steadying himself as the Ferris wheel kept turning, their cars continuing their ascent. Rhyme took the certificate and leaned down over the side of her car, digging her foot into the space beneath the bench. Blood rushed to her head. Down below was a sea of lights. Conrad stretched his hand out, his fingers a foot below Rhyme's car. *If she could just stretch a little farther . . .* The fair seemed so far away now. *A little more . . .* Conrad was on his tippy-toes now, bracing himself against the wheel. They were so high up now, nearly at the pinnacle. *Just a little more . . .*

Looking down, Rhyme and Conrad were nearly face-to-face, his arm held out to her. "Just drop the certificate," he said. "I'll catch it. I promise." Rhyme closed her eyes and let the envelope fall from her hand. When she opened her eyes, Conrad was holding the blue piece of paper. A second later, he was back in the car, giving the certificate over to Fiske. Rhyme pulled herself back up into her car, and when she got her bearings, looked down again.

That was when the Ferris wheel lurched to a stop, and Rhyme was suspended like a Christmas ornament at the highest point in Attaway.

CHAPTER 31

From far below, a familiar voice came over the loudspeaker.

"This is Matilda Higgins speaking," said the announcement, blaring across every corner of the grounds. "We are down here with the authorities—*er*, a security guard named Marvin—and will only turn this wheel back on if Fiske Quentin promises to turn himself in and release his nephew. Mr. Quentin, if you can agree to those terms, please call Meg's cell phone and let us know."

Rhyme peered over the edge to see Fiske pulling his phone from his pocket. The wind had picked up, and her car was rocking from left to right like a pendulum. She had never been particularly scared of heights, but that was quickly changing. Over the loudspeaker, Rhyme heard Fiske's terrible voice—carried, she supposed, through Matilda's phone. "I'll do no such thing," Fiske said. "This is a private matter. Family business. Start the ride back up, and we can all find an agreeable solution on the ground." Another gust of wind blew in, almost knocking Fiske off his feet.

Then, another voice came on over the speakers. "Sir, this is Silas Manderley. I understand you have a certificate for a hefty sum of money. If you agree to come down now, and leave the children unharmed, I'll happily let you keep that certificate." Manderley's voice was soothing, authoritative, and—Rhyme hoped—convincing. "Do we have a deal?"

"How do I know I can trust you?" Fiske demanded.

"On the life of Betty Cassidy, my one true love, you have my word," Manderley replied.

"Fine," said Fiske. "Bring us down."

Matilda took the phone. "Hold on, Rhyme!" she said, as the wheel sprang to life. The way down was a lot less scary than the way up. The whole time, Rhyme kept her eyes on Conrad, who stayed in his seat while Fiske stood menacingly overhead. As they tilted closer to solid ground, Rhyme saw that a crowd had gathered beneath the Ferris wheel. No doubt, the visitors had heard Matilda and Fiske over the speakers and came to watch what happened. *Ms. Sharpe was going to be so mad!* But for now, Rhyme just needed to get back on her feet—and make sure nothing happened to Conrad. She was on a level now with the tents. Twangy music was being piped through the speakers, and excited chatter from the grounds filtered upwards. Billy and Holly came into view, pointing up at her.

Ten seconds later, Rhyme was being pulled out of her car by the elderly operator, Junior, and the security guard—*he really looked like a Marvin*! They all kept asking Rhyme if she was all right, if anything was broken. "Hurry, this way," said Junior, throwing a Millwood blanket over her shoulders. "You'll be safe now." Rhyme looked up to see Matilda at the railing. Behind her, Meg stood beside Silas Manderley. Two pairs of green eyes. She was about to greet them when everyone looked up at once, in horror. Rhyme turned. Fiske, she saw, had jumped off the ledge of his car and into the darkness behind the Ferris wheel. "Argh!" she heard him scream; the fall must've been twenty feet or more.

Marvin hurried after him, down the steps and into the wilderness. Having just been stuck in the air, Rhyme knew how large the forest was, and how many places there would be for Fiske to hide. *If he hadn't broken his leg, that is . . .* More importantly, the second car had reached the platform, and the operator was helping Conrad out. He looked a little worse for the wear, but otherwise unharmed. Junior draped another blanket around his shoulders. "Rhyme!" Conrad exclaimed, and the two of them ran into each other's arms. "I'm so glad you're safe," he said. "That was a really close call." Before she could reply, the noise of the crowd seemed to explode, and suddenly everyone was crowding around them.

When she looked up, Silas Manderley and Ms. Sharpe were standing at their sides, along with Matilda and Meg.

"It's a family reunion," Silas said, as the crowd moved them toward a row of waiting police cars.

Two hours later, it was nearly midnight at the Attaway Police Station, and Rhyme and Matilda couldn't hear what was being said on the other side of the glass. They'd been at the station for two hours now, when Rhyme and Matilda were separated from the twins and Silas Manderley. Since then, Manderley had been shut in Sheriff Gibson's office, presumably explaining what had transpired that night. Both girls slumped back down onto the wooden bench. Rhyme was extraordinarily tired, and before she had time to ask the policewoman across from her for a cup of coffee, she was fast asleep.

Her dreams were strange and scattered. It was a few months ago, all over again, at State. Instead of dancing, she and the Chicken Girls were doing acrobatics, dangling from tightropes and waltzing across gym mats. Ellie was there, and Kayla and Birdie, and Quinn and Rooney. They were all wearing leotards, like the ones they'd worn as little girls. As the music picked up, they started to twist and turn in a bizarre routine. All the while, Rhyme felt an icy chill behind her, as if Fiske was still out there, at large. When the girls parted, she saw him coming toward her. T. K. *Rhyme, wake up,* he said. *It's time to go home, Rhyme. C'mon, sweetie . . .* The room was spinning like a Ferris wheel, until she opened her eyes and saw both of her parents, squatting in front of the bench, and Harmony hanging behind.

"Nothing to apologize for," her father said softly.

"That sweet girl Matilda explained everything to us," her mother said, brushing away a strand of Rhyme's hair. *Sweet girl?* Rhyme wondered if she was still dreaming.

"But Meg and Conrad and—"

"They're fine, Rhyme," Matilda said, holding her car keys. "I'm going home, too. We're invited to Mr. Manderley's house tomorrow for lunch. I'll pick you up at noon?" Rhyme nodded sleepily, wondering if she was still dreaming. Her father scooped her up like she was still a six-year-old, and her mother said, "Hush, Harmony," and sometime later she was back home, in her bed, and then it was morning.

CHAPTER 32

Through the window, Rhyme saw her dad unloading suitcases from the car. Just the sight of him, wearing the same green T-shirt he always wore on his days off, back home and in the driveway, made her choke up inexplicably. She hadn't even realized how much she had missed them.

"Heya, kiddo!" he said brightly as Rhyme ran downstairs and buried herself in his hug. She immediately began weeping. Her dad seemed surprised by her cries, muffled in the soft cotton of his shirt, but he settled into it, patting her back and trying to calm her. "You're all right now," he said. "But that was a real roller coaster ride!"

"You mean Ferris wheel," Rhyme said, pulling back with a smile, sniffling. "I'm just glad you're back. I really missed you guys." Her father looked touched, and he pulled her in for another hug before her mother came out side.

"There you are!" She came over and smothered Rhyme in an embrace. "I was so *worried*. All this business about these runaway twins and some horrible man. Apparently he's still on the run!" She looked at Rhyme's tear-streaked face and exchanged a worried look with her husband, who shook his head as if to say "It's fine." She cupped Rhyme's head in both hands and brushed dry her daughter's teary cheeks. It was remarkable how much could be fixed with a mother's touch.

"What is *this*?" Harmony said as she came out of the door, holding Meg's wide-brimmed hat. "Can I wear it? Look how fabulous I am!" She put it on and sauntered toward Rhyme. *Same old Harmony*, Rhyme thought with a grin, making up a fast excuse about buying the hat at a yard sale. She took it back when she gave Harmony a hug, telling her she wanted to hear all about Hollywood before running inside to remove any remaining items that might give Meg and Conrad away.

A couple loose socks, a white T-shirt that must be Conrad's—it smelled like him, pine needles and laundry detergent. Embroidered on the tag was Conrad's name, no doubt a relic from life with Betty. She breathed a sigh of relief that no one had noticed the items, at least not enough to pick them up and see the name.

When she came back downstairs, Rhyme was beaming. This was how it was supposed to be, she and her family, at home, together. She felt safe here in a way she never did when they were gone, especially once Fiske showed up. And now that they were back, everything would be right again. Movie nights. Stargazing. Maybe there was even still time to greet the fireflies (with an apology, of course, for their tardiness). "Can you make mac and cheese tonight, Mom?" Rhyme asked as she turned the corner into the kitchen.

Her mother nodded. "Of course, dear. But you better go upstairs and get ready. That sweet girl Matilda will be here soon!" The clock showed eleven—*how had she slept so late?* She really was becoming a teenager. . . . Upstairs, Rhyme paid particular attention to what she wore, deciding on a loose linen jumpsuit that made her feel a little glamorous. It had pockets, so she knew what to do with her hands, and every time she had worn it, she'd been complimented. In the mirror she saw a high schooler.

Matilda picked her up at twelve on the dot, and they drove in near silence up the long drive to Manderley Estate. They drove for a couple of hours—past Attaway limits, past Millwood. Rhyme had only a vague idea of where they were. Out here, there were few houses, just trees and dandelions and the narrow road. Maybe it was a bad place to live, or maybe Silas Manderley owned everything the eye could see. Still feeling a little drowsy, Rhyme rested her head against the cool window and let the sunlight dance under her eyelids. She must've drifted off again, because the next thing she heard was Matilda saying, "Wake up and smell the roses." Rubbing her eyes, Rhyme followed Matilda to the door.

"Oh, hello!" a woman said, opening the front door before Rhyme and Matilda had even knocked. From the outside, the house was impressive—dark-stained wood shingles, steep roofs of burnished copper, and a sweeping porch that wrapped all the way around the house. Gorgeous, but not ostentatious. It was unclear how large the house was, the back extending into the forest. But as they entered the main hall, the answer became clear: unfathomably enormous.

"Hello, girls," Silas Manderley said, as he'd seemingly been standing there waiting for them. "Young women, I should say." This was the first time either Rhyme or Matilda had been this close to him, and they were speechless for a second as they took it all in. Up close, he seemed the largest person in the room, calm but powerful, like an ocean. As he drew closer to extend a hand, Rhyme saw the eyes she would have recognized anywhere. They had the same piercing quality and brilliant color.

"I'm Silas. Or," he added, a wry smile that reminded Rhyme of Conrad spreading across his face, "Vincent Patterson, as I've heard you're more familiar with." Matilda and Rhyme looked at each other in disbelief. "Come with me," he said.

They followed him into a grand dining room with a vaulted ceiling, where Meg and Conrad sat, both in borrowed clothes that were clearly twelve times more expensive than anything they'd ever worn before. "Sorry we didn't wait," Conrad said, rolling up a fruit-filled crepe and stuffing it into his mouth. He'd been cleaned up at the police station, but he still had a swollen, black eye from Fiske. *Still handsome*, thought Rhyme. *I wonder if T. K. would still be handsome with a black eye?* Conrad started to say something else, but Rhyme couldn't decipher it with his mouth so full.

Meg was more reserved, and Rhyme noticed she kept looking around as if waiting for the walls to come down and cameras to come out. "Hey," was all she said.

"I'm sure you all want to hear the full story," Silas said, pulling up between Conrad and Meg. And everyone nodded. "Betty and I met at the library, if you can believe it. Millwood's own was little more than a few encyclopedias and tattered hardcovers Attaway's library had recycled out, so I went there in search of *The Stranger*—I was an H. P. Lovecraft fanatic, and she loved Tolkien, as I'm sure you know. Anyway, we began debating the merits of C. S. Lewis, whom I've always loved, and one thing led to another and . . ." He let out an involuntary sigh. "You read the letters," he finally settled on.

"Anyway, this was 1964, as you know, and times were different then." He cocked his head to the side. "Well, not all that different, unfortunately, but certainly worse, and especially for me and Betty's relationship."

"So you really were Vincent Patterson?" Matilda interjected. Of everyone, she seemed the most clearheaded and able to ask the appropriate follow-up questions.

"Yes, 'Vinny,' as she called me. She was the only one I allowed to call me that. She insisted, actually. When Betty's parents found out about us, they tried to rip us apart. Threatened her, threatened me, told me they'd report me and send me straight to jail. But it wasn't any use. *You have to go the way your blood beats. If you don't*

*live the only life you have, you won't live some other life, you won't live
any life at all.*"

"James Baldwin," Meg said. She had been reading him since
they found Vincent's senior quote, just in case it offered a further
clue.

"Yes, one of my favorites," Silas said. "I introduced her to
Baldwin's work. She used that very quote, in fact, to convince me
to continue seeing her despite the potential problems. And then she
became pregnant. Our senior year. We tried to hide it, made a plan
to run away, actually. Something you would appreciate," he said,
nodding to the twins.

They grinned sheepishly.

"But her parents caught on before we could leave, and sent her
away to the Crown Lake Sanitorium for Delinquent Girls. They
made sure I was banned from the premises, my letters to her and her
letters to me thrown away."

Silas sighed and rubbed the back of his neck like Conrad did
when he was embarrassed. But Silas seemed more ashamed, exhaling deeply before admitting, "Her parents came to me, the police
outside my door. They said that if I didn't leave Betty alone, they'd
make it their mission to make sure I never left the jail cell they were
only too eager to throw me in. 'We don't hate you, Vincent,' they
said. 'We just want what's best for our Betty. What kind of life could
she have with you? What kind of life would that baby have?'" The
table fell silent. No one spoke for several moments.

"Now, I was just an eighteen-year-old kid then, you have to remember, with barely any self-esteem. Betty *was* better than I could ever hope to get. And I *did* only want the best for her. So I believed her parents and took their $10,000. And then I signed up for the army. I had lost the love of my life, so who cared what happened to me? I had nothing to live for. When Betty returned with our—" Silas choked up and corrected himself. "With the baby, I had already been deployed. I don't blame her for never forgiving me, especially since my letters never made their way to her. Not until a few years ago, that is."

"But I'm getting ahead of myself," he said. "I fought with the 143rd Division for several years, advancing to lieutenant colonel before the Easter attack." He took a deep breath, clearly reliving several memories he didn't want to share. "All that got me through those long, horrid nights was a friendship I'd developed. With a nice young man from New York City, the heir to a railroad fortune—or so he thought. Not long before he died, a letter came, saying his father had made a series of crooked investments and the family was ruined. He and I started plotting immediately. We thought there was an opportunity to buy up local newspapers, consolidate them. His family had owned a paper in Brooklyn. We sketched together a business plan." Manderley took a deep breath and looked out the window to his vast backyard.

"Soon after," he continued, "we took a few days of heavy artillery. I got a bullet in the left leg. And then a bomb sent me fifteen yards from camp and into darkness. Half my company was wiped off the face of the earth—Silas Manderley included. I was as good as dead. And as far as the army knew, I *was* dead. DIA, they classified me," he said, which rang a bell with Rhyme.

"What's DIA?" she said, remembering the acronym next to Vincent Patterson's name at the retrospective.

"Death in absentia. It means they didn't find my body and I never surfaced, so they assumed I was dead. But this all happened without my knowledge. I was asleep, unconscious, then in and out of consciousness for what I was told was seven weeks. When I finally woke I was lost and confused. I spoke no Vietnamese. Six months later, I was back in the United States, using Silas Manderly's ID tags. In a safe deposit box, I had only one possession of any worth: the cash Betty's parents had given me. I had never touched it. I just let it sit in a bank in Millwood for all those years. So I was determined to become a man her parents would approve of, someone whose letters they would convey, someone whose life they deemed worthy of their daughter's."

"But how did you become Silas Manderley?" Conrad, now on his third Belgian waffle, interjected. "That's what I can't understand."

"Though I was a black man in America, my skin was always light," Silas explained. "I could pass. So to start my new business, I needed a name people could get behind. No one questions your money if you have a name like Silas Manderley. So under that name, I bought up my first newspaper, in Poughkeepsie, under the name of H. U. Y. Enterprises."

"Why H. U. Y.?" This time it was Matilda who interrupted.

"*Huy* was the name of my doctor overseas, a Vietnamese man. He said his name meant 'successful.' So, why not? But by the time I bought up my seventh paper, everyone was calling the company by *my* name . . . or should I say by Silas's. And that name stuck. I transformed the company into Manderley Holdings, and soon after we got into book publishing, radio, and eventually television."

"So that stock certificate we found in Betty's room?" asked Meg. "That Uncle Fiske now has?"

"It was something I sent to Betty, that I suppose her parents decided not to throw out. I'm told the authorities still haven't found your uncle, but I suspect they will. So for a few more days, he can fancy himself a millionaire."

"When did you come back home?" Rhyme said, wanting Silas to finish the story.

"I bought this house in 1987, a few years after Manderley Holdings began operations in New York. And the first thing I did was find her again. My Betty."

He cleared his throat. "I stopped by her house once, ringing the doorbell, holding a bouquet of flowers. But her husband answered the door. She had a husband. And behind him, two children. Our child and *her* child," Silas said, looking toward the twins. "Your mother. She was fifteen then, with a brother who had nothing to do with Vincent Patterson. They both called that man 'Dad.' So I made up an excuse about being a flower delivery man who had the wrong address. I left. It felt like the right decision at the time. To let her go. She moved to Asheville a couple years later."

"I had reached out to Betty finally," Silas said, "only five years ago. I had heard her husband, Al, passed—I had kept up with her over the years, not that she knew, of course—and reintroduced myself. It was only then we realized the full extent of what her parents had done. But she told me she had kept my letters after all those years, the ones that got to her before her parents got to us."

"But neither of us wanted to live in the past, though we remembered it fondly. Neither of us regret—regretted—our lives, and we maintained a lovely correspondence these last five years. So what do you think?" It took a second to realize Silas was asking a question, and Meg and Conrad looked at each other, neither knowing what that meant. "Living with me, now that your uncle, I mean—

"Of course, you don't have to," Silas said. "But if you would want to stay with me now that your grandmother is gone . . . It gets mighty lonely in this big place all alone . . ." No one dared breathe. "Her estate, of course, is yours. That is, once we find Fiske. But now that your uncle has shown his true colors it won't be hard to dissolve any paperwork he filed during Betty's final days. The house, and everything in it, will be yours in due time. Until then . . ." Silas trailed off, shifting in his seat. "I thought if you wanted to live here, I mean . . ."

"Excuse me??" Meg finally interrupted, putting down her knife and fork. Everyone turned to her.

"I shouldn't have asked, I understand." Silas said, clearly disappointed. "It is very soon, and—"

"Of course we want to live here," Meg said, breaking out one of her rare smiles. "It's about time Conrad and I get to know our grandfather."

Silas didn't blink before his eyes were streaming with tears, his face broken into a million lines from the grin that stretched from ear to ear. "Well, I'd sure like to get to know my grandkids, too, Meg."

The twins smiled at each other and at their grandfather.

CHAPTER 33

Matilda and Rhyme spent the day at Silas's with the twins, playing croquet on his court, swimming in his inground pool—both of them—and eating so many foods they couldn't pronounce that Conrad swore he would vomit. But soon, the sun was setting, and the twins and Silas were leaving the next day for Asheville.

After Silas thanked Rhyme and Matilda for their help, promising to give support if they ever needed it, the twins walked them out to Matilda's car. "We'll see each other again," Conrad said, though they knew they probably wouldn't.

"Of course," Rhyme and Meg said at the same time. Meg said bye to Rhyme first, gripping her in a tight hug and thanking her for being the coolest girl she had ever met. "You feel sort of like my little sis," Meg said at one point, and Rhyme had to hold her jaw from dropping. "Call me if you ever want to talk. You remind me a lot of myself at your age, and I'd love to help you avoid the same mistakes I made." Rhyme could feel her throat catching, so she just pulled Meg in for another hug.

Conrad rubbed the back of his neck as Rhyme peeled off from Meg and approached. "I guess now's goodbye," he said. He rolled his eyes and grinned, that infectious smile that pulled at the corners of Rhyme's mouth. "I'm gonna miss you, Rhyme. And . . ." He seemed to be struggling with how to articulate what he wanted to say next. "And whatever guy you've been texting all summer . . . If he doesn't realize how smart and special and perfect you are, then he's not worth your salt." Rhyme didn't know exactly what that meant, but she knew what Conrad was trying to say.

"I was that obvious?" Rhyme finally said, impressed at how perceptive Conrad was.

"Meg figured it out," he said, which made much more sense. Rhyme laughed, already spilling tears as she pulled him in for a hug. They all made promises to keep in touch as they separated.

Matilda and Rhyme rode home in silence, both knowing neither would ever acknowledge this experience at school, but also that they shared something secret. Something special.

When Rhyme got home, her house was empty. "Mom? Dad? Harmony?" she called out, reviving the fear she thought she'd put to bed. Had Uncle Fiske come back for one final blow? But she heard a whistle, her father calling her out back, where he stood grilling burgers and veggies and wearing the ratty Kiss the Cook apron she didn't remember him ever not having.

"What's going on?" Rhyme said, as she saw a tray of jars on the outdoor table. Harmony already had one in her hand, chasing a blinking light that rose out of reach.

"We're celebrating your passing the Test Test," her mother said, not able to feign casualness long before running to Rhyme and grabbing her in an ecstatic hug. "The school just called!" Rhyme didn't know what to say, she had completely forgotten about the test.

"We're also catching up with the fireflies," Rhyme's father said, as if it were obvious. "They're very upset we didn't properly greet them this summer." Rhyme's eyes, which seemed like faucets today, ran over as she grabbed a jar.

"Well then, we *must* make it up to them," she said, brushing her hair out of her eyes as she joined her sister catching fireflies.

EPILOGUE

A few days later, Rhyme was walking Reggie when a brightly painted bus full of screaming girls drove by before screeching to a halt. Out bounded several girls with duffel bags and suntans and friendship bracelets. Leading the pack were Ellie and Kayla, followed by Quinn. Neither Rhyme nor the girls could speak for the first several minutes, just grabbing and looking at each other and then screaming before repeating the cycle.

"I'm so happy to see you guys," Rhyme finally said as the street-lights turned on. "I really missed you." They exchanged another round of hugs before Ellie and Kayla launched into a detailed description of their summer at camp, which had involved a lot of bonding with PowerSurge, a reality almost stranger than the one Rhyme had lived.

"So how was your summer?" Ellie finally asked, and Rhyme walked several paces as she considered her response.

"Nothing special," she said. "Pretty much as boring as expected." Rhyme smiled to herself as they moved onto discussing plans for dance team next year. Even if she had told them the truth, they never would have believed her.

About the Author

Matilda Higgins is the former editor-in-chief of the *Attaway Appeal* and an aspiring novelist and historian. She helped Ms. Sharpe, the Attaway librarian, create an incredible historical exhibit for the county fair. She's the youngest of five daughters and an eighth generation Attawinian. In her spare time, Matilda competes in triathlons and scours the town for a new lead. She hopes to matriculate to NYU and study journalism. This is her debut novel.